MY FATHER, M

JULIANE, DAU

BY J.P. REEDMAN

Table of Contents

I was born a King's daughter…but I swear by all that is Holy, the Virgin's Milk, the fragments of the True Cross, a spike from Jesu's Crown of Thorns, that I wish the man who begot me had not worn a fancy crown or wielded a wrathful blade. I'd rather have had a lowly but kind-hearted peasant for my sire; a loyal man who went home from tilling his fields with good, clean soil upon his hands, not the blood of others.

Had a simple man begot me, I, too, would have known a simple life and eventually married a good-souled farmer, smith or potter, who would have given me a gaggle of children to gladden my heart and, in the course of time, present me with their own winsome babes—my legacy to the world, my blood passed on forever.

But such a life was not to be. A King's daughter I was born, even if born on the wrong side of the blanket, and my only legacy will be one of infamy. From the day of my birth, the die was cast…

My gaze is drawn down the corridor of the great Abbey of Fontevraud, candle-lit, haunted by shadows and black-clad nuns shuffling by like the shades of the departed. Monstrous carved faces, beaked and toothed, glare down from the capitals of the cloister pillars; the air reeks of tallow, faint incense and the musky fug of too many unwashed bodies.

Out of the gloom, they totter towards me, silent, swift—two nuns, side by side, shoulders touching, robes mingling with robes so that they almost seem twins conjoined. They hold wooden staves on which they lean like old crones, feeling the flagstones for cracks and crannies that might trip them. They are dressed a little differently to myself and other the nuns; the same austere black habit, the same stark urine-bleached wimple, but their faces are masked by pale linen bands with crude slits cut out at the level of mouth and nose. The linen looks oddly flat, featureless, glowing faint yellow-white in the candle-glow, giving their faces the semblance of skulls.

As the nuns approach, they halt as if sensing my presence. They are like animals that way. Swallowing, I clutch my rosary beads and pray, saying nothing.

I dare not speak. Would they? I always hoped against hope…

The two nuns say nothing. They journey on toward the doorway of the Chapter House, tapping the flooring with their staves. I breathe a sigh of relief but continue to pray as tears drip down my cheeks.

They are both blind.

The nuns are my daughters, Lora and Peronelle. Years ago, their eyes had been put out. Their noses had been slit.

Henry, first of that name, King of England, Duke of Normandy, had allowed their mutilation. Countenanced it. Their grandfather—my royal sire of whom I had once been so proud.

No mother could ever love the man who harmed her children, even if he was her own Father who God says must be obeyed and honoured.

And so, long before I retired to Fontevraud to seek peace and solace, I tried to kill the King of England…

CHAPTER ONE

My mother was named Ansfrida and she was one of Henry Beauclerc's many mistresses. From the time he reached maturity, my father took the summons of the Bible to 'go forth and multiply' with great seriousness, albeit he ignored the other exhortations to be chaste outside the marriage bed. Oddly, he produced but two children with his wedded wife, Edith, later named Matilda, the Good Queen, but with his concubines his children were legion—of daughters there were three Matildas, Sybil and Sybilla, Constance, Mabel, Alix, Isabel, Adeliza, Gundreda, Rohese and Emma; of sons, two Roberts, one now Earl of Gloucester, Reginald, now Earl of Cornwall, Gilbert, Henry and my own brothers, Fulk and Richard.

I was called Juliane, after Saint Julian the Hospitaller.

Mama was an Englishwoman of Saxon blood. She was tall and rosy-cheeked with light brown braids that hung to her waist and a buxom, womanly figure that attracted many men. At the age of fourteen she wed the knight Anskill, a tenant of Abingdon Abbey; together, they produced a son called Guillaume, a surprising choice of name for those of Saxon descent, but then my mother was always looking to better herself in the world, and in that world the lords from Normandy ruled supreme. Unfortunately, Anskill was imprisoned by my father's elder brother, the reviled William Rufus, and died after harsh treatment in the Red King's dungeons.

So mama was left a young, pretty widow. And it was while she prayed at the unfortunate Anskill's tomb in Abingdon Abbey that young Henry, not a King then, of course, noticed her—and she noticed him. With a young son to care for and little money left to her by her dead husband, she knew the only course she could take.

Within the week, she was romping in young Henry Beauclerc's bed. Within the month, she was installed as his mistress in a fine manor just outside Lincoln. She was one of his favourite concubines, too, I am told, her clear blue eyes and ample curves holding strong attraction. I was the youngest child of her union with Henry, born after Fulk and then Richard.

After King William died, shot in the heart by an arrow in the New Forest, my father became King of England. Some claimed he'd paid for his brother to be murdered while on the hunt; I cannot pretend Henry was not ruthless enough to do so. It was certainly odd that he was lingering in the forest that same day the King was slain, although not in the King's company—it was also odd how the news reached him so swiftly and how he never rushed to his stricken brother's side despite his close proximity. Instead, he went riding in all haste for Winchester where he claimed the treasury—and the crown.

Once his Coronation was performed, my early life became one of privilege. I learnt not just the womanly arts of sewing, embroidery, dancing and household management but also to read and to speak fluently in Norman French. "You will marry a fine lord one day, Juliane," Mama would say, fussing over my snarled, elf-locked hair and straightening my rumpled bliaut. "You must not forget how fortunate you are. When I met your father, he was royal but just a younger son, until God passed judgment on wicked William, who is to blame for my husband Anskill's death."

Tirel's arrow, fired carelessly or perhaps with deadly purpose on Father's orders, was the true cause of King William's demise, I always wanted to say, and if Rufus had not injured Anskill unto death, Mama would not have bedded Henry and borne him three children, but I feared I'd get a thrashing for my impertinence. Mama would hear nought said against her beloved Henry, ignoring his cruelties as well as his scores of willing bedfellows. Walter Tirel, who fired the fatal bolt would not speak of what had taken place within the forest; he had fled to France, which, in many eyes, made him look guilty indeed.

Having two older brothers and no young females as friends (Guillaume, my half-brother, had entered the church), I was rather an unruly hoyden—climbing trees in the orchard, dressing in boys' hose when mother was not around and rampaging through the nearby wood with Fulk and, pretending we were on a boar hunt. Fiercely I jabbed my makeshift spear into the foliage, hoping to smite some fell beast—if not a great boar with gore-stained tusks, then a cockatrice or a troll...

Such childish folly soon passed, however, as it always must. I began to grow tall and my body sprouted in many ways. Fulk and Richard became embarrassed to be seen in my company. Mama now insisted I stay in the solar of our manor house and practice my sewing. I hated sewing and I hated even more that I was so big in size—I outstripped mother by a head in height and even topped my father, who was burly and robust rather than tall.

"You have the blood of the Saxons in you, Juliane," sighed Mama, looking me over with critical eyes. "Your great-grandfather towered over lesser men like a great tree, and had eyes like blue lances, keen and all-seeing, yet kind. His name was Nothelm. He fought—and died—at Senlac, defending his King."

I had no care for old stories and wondered why Mama bothered to tell them. Remote Saxon ancestors, no matter how brave, held no interest. The Normans ruled England; I knew no other life save the one beneath their rule. And I *was* half-Norman and a King's byblow besides. I was aware of where my loyalties must lie to get along in the world. But it was depressing when the ideal lady was considered to be petite, blonde and demur. I fit none of those specifications with the raven hair I had inherited from my royal sire, my gangly, looming height and my somewhat thorny temper. In moments of youthful angst, I would even throw myself onto my pallet, crying, "By God's Teeth, I am so plain, I will surely end up a cloistered nun!" and had Mama and my nurse running around in dismay, attempting to console or cajole me to better moods.

But soon such youthful follies and my simple childhood life came to an end. On my sixteenth birthday, a messenger from King Henry arrived at the manor. As the courier rode into the courtyard on a huge bay steed, I guessed at once he came on official business; he and his band of travelling companions bore the lion of the Duchy of Normandy on their surcoats.

Wearing her best bliaut and all the accumulated gems father had presented her so that she glimmered and flickered as she moved, Mama emerged from the doorway to greet the newcomers. The messenger dismounted and gave a brief bow as if Mama was an actual lady, not just a King's concubine. However, as she listened to the words the messenger read from a scroll, her face became grave and she beckoned him into the hall for more privacy.

Lurking near our little stable where I had been feeding my white pony Lucia, I sulked, for I was not privy to the news, whatever it was. Folding my arms crossly, I flung myself down on a stack of dry hay. I convinced myself the news the courier brought was bad—Father had not visited in person for ages; I suspected, with the frank pessimism of a sullen adolescent, that he was wearying of Mama and spending his time begetting scores of other royal bastards elsewhere. Soon, I imagined, he would push some fine Norman in her direction and expect them to wed. Mama would comply, of course, as it was the way of most mistresses, and she'd most likely receive a decent pension that would keep her and any new husband comfortable till the end of their days...

As for me, well, I considered myself near enough an old maid now. Half the girls my age in the local village were wed or betrothed; some even had swelling bellies or new-born babes. Despite Mama telling me what a catch I was, no names of prospective suitors had ever arisen, and it was Father's prerogative to bestow my hand where he felt it might help his cause. He was taking so long to decide, I was certain my angst-laden screeching about being forced into the cloister would surely come true...

Shoes sounded on cobblestones. I glanced up from my unhappy reverie to see Mama rapidly approaching the open stable door, her veil flying out in the breeze. "Juliane..." she gasped, entering the darkness of the stable. She stooped, swaying as if she might faint.

Now I began to think of even more unpleasant possibilities. Perhaps the King was cutting off all ties for some imagined or invented offence, perhaps he had fared into the forest on a hunt like the unfortunate William Rufus and met the same fate...

"Mother, what is the matter? Tell me! You are as white as curdled milk!" Leaping up from the straw, I grasped at her sleeve, dislodging a little gem sewn on the cuff. She did not even look down as the precious gewgaw rolled away.

"The time has come," she said breathlessly and suddenly her eyes dampened and she gathered me in a hard embrace. "His Grace the King is in Winchester and asks that you attend upon him there. He is soon faring to Normandy—and before he goes, he has glad news to impart to you. My dearest daughter, at last all my hopes for your future have come to pass. The King has finally bothered to find you a fitting husband. You are to be married."

Abruptly I pulled away from her, my mouth gaping open like that of a simpleton. For all my endless moaning about my unwed state, the sudden idea of wedding some stranger struck me like a physical blow. It was the way things were done in high circles but—but what if the chosen man was ugsome and smelly, or old and toothless; what if he were quick with his fists or mean with money?

Mother was pushing me towards the stable door. "You are to go straight to Winchester in the company of the messenger. I must search out your best gown. I beg you make me proud, Juliane. Act as a lady should—none of this prideful nonsense so many young maids indulge in. And remember me to your royal father—let him know I miss him dearly and would fain see him soon."

Winchester was a glorious sight to a girl who had only travelled to Lincoln a few times and spent the rest of her time in a village. Great walls surrounded the city, towered and gated, and the music of the great cathedral bells of the New Minster and St Swithun's Abbey pealed out over the thriving market place and merchants' houses. I had expected to be carried hence in a litter, as a princess, but no such transportation had been supplied; I rode a horse instead, which did not truly bother me, as I was always stronger and more active than most girls my age and enjoyed the freedom of the ride.

In my long, woollen blue cloak and with a light veil on my head that barely concealed the raven tumble of my hair, I proceeded through the town with pride. After a short while, I noticed the men and women in the street staring and pointing.

I realised they had deduced I was someone of note, although it was quite clear they knew not who. My chin tilted up, I straightened my back and basked in their perceived admiration.

Only it was *not* admiration.

"Look at the strumpet!" I heard someone cry, the voice full of loathing and mockery. "One of the King's doxies being taken to the palace."

Stunned, I stared into the crowd. Far from gazing upon my person with approval and delight, I saw a sea of hostile faces swimming in my direction. Bawling women in shaggy shawls; men in rough homespun hoods who spat and gesticulated.

My father's men in their lion-blazoned tabards drew their swords, warning the milling throng that their behaviour would not be tolerated.

"You do wrong to Matilda, the Good Queen!" screeched one old woman, her mouth a toothless cavern and hairs bristling like spikes on her chin. "Shame on you, hussy! Shame, shame!" Reaching down into the teeming gutter, she grabbed a ball of unmentionable slime and hurled it in my direction, even as one of my guards spurred his horse towards her, weapon upraised.

She fled into the crowds; her obscene missile struck my ankle, soiling the hem of my best gown as it splattered. A rotten reek filtered upwards to assail my nostrils. Anger flooded my being at my undeserved treatment but I was shocked and upset too—tears prickled my eyes, making my vision hazy. I had harmed no one, yet everyone seemed to despise me.

"Mistress Juliane, do not fear." One of the King's men took hold of my horse's bridle, guiding the beast forward; it was growing skittish now, unnerved by the crowd. "We will take you out of harm's way."

Mercifully the entrance to Winchester Castle was not far ahead. As I rode dejectedly under the shadow of its great white towers, relief flooded me—but it soon turned to fear. What of 'Good Queen' Matilda, so loved by the people of England for her good works and generosity. She was here in residence with the King, having not long given birth to his heir, William Adelin. Would Matilda, like the townsfolk who loved her, despise me—the product of her husband's numerous infidelities?

I had no more time to ponder the matter. Dismounting my horse, I found myself approached by a brisk-mannered chamberlain and chivvied along towards the castle's great hall. I tried to protest, for my gown was a rancid disgrace and my face still flushed with embarrassment, but the bald, nervous, impolite little man ignored my protest.

I was almost bodily pushed into the smoky hall, full of courtiers, servants and supplicants, and stood there, as dumb as a sheep, holding up my drenched and stinking skirts, my hair straggling under my now-twisted veil. After a moment of noisy throat-clearing, the chamberlain roared out my name: "Mistress Juliane FitzRoy!"

Heads swivelled in my direction; there was no escaping my fate, whatever it was to be. Head bowed, attempting to hide my blushes, I trudged over the rush-strewn tiles and curtseyed before the two thrones set up on a high dais at the far end of the room.

My father sat on one, a golden circlet on his brow, a furred robe around his shoulders. He looked much as I remembered from his last visit to Mama's manor—burly, brawny, with a red, rugged face and wiry near-black hair that held a touch of flame where the torchlight stroked it. On the other seat was the 'Good Queen' Matilda, whose birth name was Edith but who had been given a more suitable Norman name at her Coronation. She was not Norman, of course—her father Malcolm of Scotland, her mother Margaret a Princess of the old English kingdom of Wessex. Some men claimed she was plain, perhaps to explain my father's fascination with other women's beds, but I found her a plump yet beauteous woman, her face smooth and pale as cream, great necklaces of gems spilling over a bosom that strained against her deep blue gown. It was said her marriage to Father was a close one, despite his many indiscretions; the courtiers even sniggeringly nicknamed the royal couple 'Godric and Godiva,' for their easy way with both Normans and the English. I wondered why the King was content with Matilda in all ways but the marriage bed, but who was I, an innocent maid, to ponder on the carnal whims of Kings…or men in general?

"Juliane—my dearest daughter!" Father's voice thundered from the dais, making me wince a little with its gruff loudness. "How she has grown since last I beheld her! A woman grown! Is she not fair to the eye? Takes after her mother in her looks—save for the hair. That dark hair is from her sire; no doubt about it. And the nose, *my* nose.

With a nose of such *outstanding* shape, Juliane's paternity could never be in question!"

My heart sank. The whole court now knew my identity and that I was a royal bastard. It was not the worst thing in the world but such a bold announcement in front of a gathered assembly was not an event I'd envisioned, especially with pious Queen Matilda present. But even worse, Father had also implied I had a big nose like his own! Self-consciously, my hand drifted up to touch my nose. It *wasn't*; surely, he was merely teasing me!

He had not finished making me squirm, either. "Ah, and what has happened to your gown, daughter—have you been rolling in the pig-sty?" he asked with a laugh and pointed to my stinking dress, stained from the dung the evil-minded hag had hurled in the street.

The courtiers all laughed, eager to please their monarch by acting as if his every word was one of exceeding wit and genius. I saw no such brilliance, just a man who had clearly imbibed rather a lot of wine.

"No, Sire," I said, rather frostily. "It was done by one of your subjects in this very town. Because she thought I was a whore."

Henry stopped and suddenly his visage became suffused with blood. He banged his goblet down on the arm of his throne. The jolly monarch of a few moments before had vanished utterly. "This woman will be found; she will be whipped for her insolence."

It was not what I wanted nor expected. I had merely voiced my disappointment at my treatment in Winchester. The last thing I desired was violence over an event that was rude but trivial. What I *truly* wanted was an end to being stared at by the court, and an opportunity to change my ruined dress instead of listening to the King's jibes about it.

"My Lord King," I said, trying to keep the trembling from my voice, "the old woman does not matter. I am here in Winchester at your summons and that alone is of importance."

Good Queen Matilda turned slowly to her husband; her white fingers touched his arm. "Listen to your daughter's words and do not stir yourself to anger, your Grace. Gossips will always be gossips; their punishment will come by God's hand. Let us not dwell on unpleasantries but rather on the well-being of your child, Juliane, who has ridden many miles to be here, eschewing the gentler travel in litter or chariot that ladies are more often used to."

The anger slowly drained from my father's face; indeed, he began to look rather bored. I was a moment's trivial entertainment; my appearance had caused a brief flurry of interest amongst the barons and knights. Now they were back to more 'important' manly things—drinking, eating and discussing lands, campaigns and other such activities.

"Have your ladies take her to receive refreshment," he said to the Queen, and he waved his hand at me in dismissal and shoved a gravy-laden chicken leg into his mouth.

Two women who hovered near the dais spoke briefly to Queen Matilda and then drifted towards me, glimmering in their matching robes of white samite. "Come with us, Lady," they said deferentially—which I found rather pleasing, as I had no title then, not even 'Lady.' "We will take you to the Queen's own chambers and see to your needs."

I curtseyed to the King and Queen in turn and then let the ladies-in-waiting lead me away into the vast bulk of Winchester castle. The cool air rushing down the winding halls bathed my hot face and made me feel less fretful and unnerved. Yet I could not quite cease worrying. The Queen seemed kind but she was inviting me, the child of her rival, to her private chambers. The fruit of her husband's endless lust—surely my presence would be a source of shame to her.

I swallowed. It was foolish but my head spun with tales I had grown up with, of Saxon queens who murdered their step-sons or the prospective suitors of their daughters. Suddenly I wished I had not come to Winchester, but how could I have defied the orders of the King? Impossible. My fate was mapped out, for good or for ill.

The two handmaidens beckoned me into the Queen's sumptuous apartments. A great bed stood in one corner, draped in golden cloths. Mats of fresh rushes bound with dried flowers added warmth to the chilly floor. Red and green painted chests and tables were neatly stacked on one side; a gilded oak carving of the Virgin hung on a white-washed wall over-painted with zigzags of yellow and azure. A great shield hanging above the bed showed Henry's Lions. They weren't rampant but it seemed to me they gazed hungrily down at the covers below.

The ladies-in-waiting looked me over in silence, measuring me up with their eyes; I felt my ears start to burn with embarrassment.

"Did you bring any raiment with you, Lady?" one asked politely at length.

I had indeed, but no one seemed to know where my small ash-wood travelling chest had vanished in the confusion of my arrival. Images of greedy and dishonest stableboys and spit-turns going through my paltry items tumbled through my head. I gazed at the ladies-in-waiting and shrugged helplessly.

"Never mind," said the elder of the two, a thin woman with close- set steel-blue eyes. "Her Grace is most generous. She already said that we could find attire from the wardrobe if your own clothes were not…suitable."

I flushed to the roots of my hair. The comments made me feel like some bumpkin, unkempt and embarrassing. I even began to wonder if my things had been shunted away because they were deemed inappropriate at court—poor, embarrassing possessions unfitting for a King's daughter, even an illegitimate one. My fingers knotted together, twining nervously; I hated myself for my show of weakness. I was no wilting flower but I was beyond my area of comfort here.

"I am Yvanne," said the thin woman, who then gestured to her younger companion, "and this is Helie. "You need not see us as enemies; we will help you. Won't we, Helie?"

The other lady-in-waiting nodded. "I am going to find some garments for Mistress Juliane now." She rustled out of the chamber in a swish of green skirts.

"I cannot take such a rich gift as a gown," I said to Yvanne, trying to keep some semblance of pride.

"Well…" a mocking little smile curved the edge of her mouth, "you can hardly be in the Queen's presence in what you are currently wearing, can you?" She gestured with a languid hand to my soiled garments.

Again, my face burned. "No…I suppose you are right, Lady Yvanne. But how will I wear garments not tailored for me?"

"Helie and I have keen eyes for such things. You are a little taller than I but somewhat more…How shall I say it? More blessed with *prominent* feminine attributes! One of my gowns will suit well enough with adjustments; Helie and I are both expert seamstresses and can let it out where needed. Your under-kirtle, I take it, is undamaged by the fracas in the street?"

Silently, I nodded. The hem of the garb lying nearest my skin was dusty and dirty but it would do. I dared not ask Helie for more; I'd truly seem a rag-tag beggar.

Helie returned, carrying a light green-grey gown draped over her arm. "I am not sure about the colour suiting your complexion," said Yvanne, and once again, I was mortified, thinking of how much time I'd spent outside, not bothering to shield myself from the sun. I was brown as a berry next to the white pallor of the Queen's ladies.

Yvanne shook the dress out. Held it up against me, and sighed. "But never mind…At least it does not stink like a cow-byre."

Queen Matilda came in late in the evening. Yvanne and Helie and three other attendant ladies lit tapers everywhere, filling the room with a warm, homely orange glow. As Matilda entered, I sank into the lowest curtsey possible, hiding as best I could the scuffed hem of my under- kirtle.

Yvanne opened a clever little folding chair, which would be taken across country when the Queen travelled on her progresses around England, and laid a thick, gold-trimmed cushion upon it. Carefully Matilda sat down and the ladies removed her wimple and began to comb out her hair with bone-combs inlaid with tiny gems. Her hair was the palest yellow, almost white, falling in thick waves to her waist. Sun on snow was what it reminded me of.

Again, I was struck by such unique looks and marvelled that the King would neglect her bed for others. My mother Ansfrida was undeniably an attractive woman, but her teeth had a small gap in front and her hair was more the hue of cattle-trampled wheat than white-gold, if I was honest.

Suddenly I realised I was staring. It was not permitted to look directly at a royal unless invited to do so, and I had been gawping like a brainless ninny. Shuffling uncomfortably, I looked down at my feet.

"Are you afraid of me, Juliane?" asked the Queen in her calm, gentle voice.

"No…" I began, alarmed that I was so transparent, and then, realising I had truly been unmasked, "yes…yes, your Grace. A little."

"You need not be. I bear you no ill will…"

"But your Grace, I am…"

"My husband's bastard. Yes, I know. Henry's indiscretions matter nought to me anymore, child. Some of the boys even dwell here at court along with Matilda, my sweet namesake—one of your half-sisters. It is not for me to judge the King; that is God's right and His alone. I look only to my own soul and in my heart I find forgiveness."

I was embarrassed then that I had thought she might hate me or even do me harm. I was just one of many, after all.

"Come, sit at my side, child," she offered. Obediently, I went to Matilda and Helie pushed a stool over for me to sit upon.

"You are fair," she said, observing me closely. "Not in the traditional way but your features are good, your teeth white, and your hair like A raven's wing. I think you will make a good wife. Were you informed about the King's choice of husband for you?"

Miserably I shook my head. "I know nothing of his identity, your Grace…Please tell me, I beg you, he's not old, is he? Not old enough to be my father?"

The Queen's laughter rang out, high and clear like the pealing of the cathedral bells.

"No, no, you have no fear of becoming an old man's bride. Your betrothed's name is Eustace de Breteuil and he is of similar age."

"I do not recognise the name. Is he not one of the King's men in England?" My heart started to thud against my ribs.

Queen Matilda shook her head, the frost-pale hair surrounding her smooth, round face fanning out in a great halo as the torchlight stroked it. "No, he is in Normandy, although he is the grandson of the great William FitzOsbern, Earl of Hereford. His father, also called

William, died…and the English and Welsh lands passed to William's younger brother, Roger."

"To the younger brother? Why so?" I frowned. "Why should Eustace not have them all if he is his father's son?"

Matilda laughed again. "Oh my, young Juliane, you are as acquisitive as your sire can be on occasion! Eustace's assumption of Breteuil and the honour of Pacy was a very generous gift. You see, Eustace is a bastard. Considerable argument ensued after his father's demise as to who would rule Breteuil but, in the end, the barons agreed it should be Eustace, who is of good Norman stock, unlike the Bretons and Burgundians who desired to claim it. He is still young and will have to rely on advisors until he is fully of age, but it seems the complainants have vanished, at least for now."

I was silent. A bastard like me—but a wealthy bastard with his own lands and supporters. If he had been landless, I would have felt insulted that baseborn child was bound to baseborn child with no hope of betterment, but it seemed he held some promise for future greatness. And why not? After all, my grandsire William, known as Conqueror, was also born on the wrong side of the sheets to the daughter of a humble tanner, and he had risen in might to become King of England.

"Is this Eustace here at court, your Grace?" I asked, my heart suddenly lurching. "Has he come to claim me?"

"No, I am afraid he is still in Normandy with his tutors, learning the ways of lordship."

Disappointment ate away at me, and new fear grew in my heart too. "I…I suppose this means I must leave England!" I gasped, my head reeling with the shock. If I went to Normandy, I might never see my mother again, or my two hard-headed brothers with their horses and hounds. Never again see the rolling fields near our little manor, ripe with corn; never watch the summer sunlight bounce off the steeple of the parish church or see the quiet local stream swell to a raging torrent after the winter thaw.

"It is a wife's duty, to go where her husband is." The Queen folded her hands primly in her lap. "If the weather holds, the King will send you to Lord Eustace within a fortnight. That is why I asked for you to be brought to my chambers. I wanted to warn you, to prepare you for your future as a wife in Normandy." She smiled, her teeth like little round pearls against her red lips. "Knowing Henry, he would have just packed you off to Eustace of Breteuil as he might send the gift of a horse…"

"A horse!" I gasped, horrified. My father saw me as no better than a beast?

"Do not be offended," said Matilda. "It is just his way. He is, after all, but a man. A man who loves women but in truth knows them not at all."

CHAPTER TWO

Queen Matilda and her ladies proved kind indeed in the days that followed. My paltry travelling chest was recovered—to my surprise, the contents were intact—and another, larger one replaced it. My decent kirtles and over-gowns were placed inside along with several dresses Yvanne and Helie had adjusted with their skilful sewing needles. They even found a lady to accompany me to Normandy as my servant; she was ancient, a shrewd old creature called Gundrada who had no living kin and was out for one last adventure.

The Queen also introduced me to my shy half-sister, one of the many Matildas, who, since she dwelt at court, seemed to be one of my father's favoured byblows. Slightly younger than me she was also set to marry a Norman lord later in the year. Her betrothed was Count Rotrou of Perche, an older man with notable military experience. Thin and golden-haired, showing the lineage of her Saxon mother Editha, Matilda had earnest blue eyes the hue of cornflowers and a delicate rosebud mouth. I'd almost have been jealous if she was not my sister and, seemingly, a nice girl.

"When I heard you were coming to court, Juliane, I broidered a kerchief for you," she said. She handed me a lavender-coloured cloth, rich with needlework. Hounds chased a hare around the edge and a unicorn danced with a lion in the centre.

"Thank you, Matilda, it is beautiful."

"Call me Tilda. There are so many Matildas and Maudes in our family."

"True…but only one Juliane," I laughed.

"Yes, only one Juliane—who, I hope, will become my friend."

"Without a doubt; we are blood, but soon, I fear, I must leave for Normandy…and my wedding to the Count of Breteiul."

"Yes, and by the end of the year, I will have followed you to Normandy to wed Rotrou. A pity we could not have travelled together for comfort."

"Yes." I hung my head. "At least I have old Gundrada to console me—but that's not saying much. A girl my own age would be a better companion."

"Maybe we can meet once we both are settled in Normandy," Tilda said dubiously, "if our husbands will allow it."

"I will ask mine, I swear it, and make him agree to a meeting," I said. "Sisters should not be kept apart."

"I wish Father had brought you to court with me," Tilda sighed. "I grew up in a small village in Devon, living quietly with my mam, Editha—then suddenly when I was six the King came to look at me and he dandled me on his knee and said he had plans for my future. Without another word, I was brought in amongst all these high and mighty folks at court, with their intrigues and haughty ways. It took a long time to adjust. I was teased about my country ways by other noble children, even though the Queen was kind and saw that nothing was lacking in my education."

"I always *wanted* to come to court," I murmured, "but perhaps…perhaps my temperament would have caused me trouble. I suppose the King could not have too many bastard daughters running about to give him grief!"

Tilda laughed. "I like you, Juliane. Juliane the One and Only. Oh, do promise me, you'll visit me in Perche! Rotrou is a great warrior, by all accounts, but he's been married before and he is old, so old…" The blue eyes abruptly darkened with tears.

I clasped her little, lily-pale hand in my larger sunburnt one. "I promise…Tilda. Sister."

On the final day before my departure from Winchester, the Queen presented me a silver circlet studded with seven blue gems to wear upon my brow at my wedding. "Oh, your Grace, you are too kind," I murmured, kneeling and kissing her plump white fingers in gratitude.

"I was young once too and know how hard it can be to leave all you have known behind to wed a man of whom you know but little. I grew up in a convent at Romsey under the guidance of my aunt, the Abbess Cristina, and although I had no wish to join the Order, I was equally afraid, at first, of taking a husband. When I heard that Henry's brother Rufus had expressed an interest in my hand, horror gripped me; he would have made a terrible husband, I am sure. He hated the church and looted monasteries, and some claim he had unholy...*tastes*. Henry, when he assumed the throne, was by far the better option, and my heart warmed toward marriage. He was, and is, a chaser of women, yes, but he is a man of intellect too—they called him Beauclerc, for he can write in French, Latin and even English!"

"Some still call him Beauclerc."

"And so they do. It is his great learning that makes our marriage harmonious, even if it fails in other ways. I pray you will find common ground with your new husband too, Juliane, and in due time bear him handsome children with the blood royal running in their veins. My position as Queen is unassailable, no matter where Henry's heart and loins find fulfilment, because I have done the greatest deed a consort can do—I have given my lord a son and heir, your half-brother, William Adelin. I hope that he will grow in wisdom and help heal the rift between Norman and Saxon, for his blood is both. That is why he is surnamed 'Adelin'—it is the Norman form of the English 'Atheling', a prince."

"I hope one day it will be so, your Grace, for on my mother's side I am also of the old blood of England."

"It will come one day," said Matilda reassuringly. "Maybe not in our lifetime but perhaps when my children or their children are grown. My descendants will be peacemakers one day...I pray." She sighed, looking wistful; how unlikely her hopes seemed in the current world of sword and castle, where brother murdered brother and father hated son.

"Women are always the peace-weavers," she continued slowly, as if trying to convince herself. "Is it not so? My daughter, little Adelaide, born last year, will fill that role through a fitting marriage; she is already a bright and active girl whom the nurses find a handful!"

"I am sure it will be as you wish, your Grace," I murmured. I was not sure at all. Little Adelaide, still in swaddling, would no doubt get contracted to a foreign prince by the time she was knee-high and journey over the Narrow Sea, never to see England or her kinfolk again—just as I would fare within the next few days, riding in a ship over the stormy waves. We were little better than kine, in some ways; we wove ties that bound with our bodies but our sacrifices were often forgotten and our alliances rendered useless by violent men.

I tried to blink back the tears that filled my eyes as I suddenly thought of Mama. I wanted so much to say farewell once more, to hold her close. But there was nought I could do. The course of my life was determined by my sire's regal blood. One could not stay a child forever.

"Highness, may I make one request before I depart on the morrow?" I asked, voice tremulous.

"You may. What do you need? More cloaks? Mint to freshen the breath and calm the stomach on the sea? A fur for your litter?"

"I just wish...to write a letter to my mother, Ansfrida. I will need a scribe's assistance; I can write a little but am not as learned as my father the King. I want to find...the right words."

The Queen smiled gently at me; gems danced on her throat, green and red. "I will call for my secretary at once, Juliane. Your mother will receive her letter."

I left Winchester the next day, this time riding in a litter hung with silky drapes the colour of a dove's breast. Tilda had come down from the solar to give me a parting gift of sugared figs in a small silk pouch, while Helie and Yvanne had waved from a high window, well aware that all the knights in the castle bailey were admiring them. My new maid, old Gundrada, looked up at the women and muttered about 'a lack of morals' before clambering into the litter and making herself comfortable after a fair amount of groaning and shuffling about.

A company of my father's soldiers then surrounded the litter as protection against outlaws on the road There were joined by a contingent of warriors sent from my husband-to-be, Eustace—hard-faced men with unflattering old-style Norman hair, where the back of the neck was shaved bare.

I thought of the letter I'd sent to Mama, thanks to Queen Matilda; my mother could only read a little in her Psalter but I supposed the local priest could be trusted to read the missive out to her. There was nothing subversive in it anyway, save the teardrops that splashed it and marred the ink as Matilda's scribe penned my heartfelt farewells while I peered over his shoulder and wept...

My mood lightened as my entourage journeyed from Winchester to the port of Southampton; peering through the litter's dove-grey drapes, I savoured the sharp scent of the sea and took in the alien sights of the coastal town—sailors with roughened tanned-leather faces, loud-voiced fish-wives with wiry salt-stiffened hair, silver-scaled mackerel shining in woven baskets, urchins playing with severed fish-heads in clogged gutters, banners and ship's riggings fluttering and flailing in the wind.

What I did not savour was the sight of bunched black clouds on the horizon, their edges limned with yellow. The sky around them had taken on a sickly hue. Even as I watched them boil and twist like some living thing spawned by hell, lightning speared through the uppermost tiers. A blast of wind, oddly warm and smelling of imminent rain, blasted into my face.

Sticking my head brazenly outside of the hangings of the litter, uncaring that the fish-wives ceased to hawk their wares and cackled at me like demented witches, I called out to the leader of my entourage: "You, sir. Will it be safe for us to sail? The wind is rising."

The man shaded his eyes with a long, weathered hand and glanced at the clouds massed along the horizon. Thunder rumbled in the distance. "It will be for the ship's captain to decide, Lady, but if we hang back in Southampton, fearing the worst, who knows—we could end up stuck here for weeks, if not months. We are coming to the time of the year when the weather grows fickle and the crossing uncertain."

Feeling a little sick to my belly, I sank back into the litter. Pulling a fur around my shoulders, I glanced over at Gundrada, half-asleep, little inelegant snores emanating from her sparsely-toothed mouth. For the dozenth time, I wished Father has sent Tilda with me instead. Gundrada, I gathered, would serve as a respectable chaperone who would let no man impugn my honour, but she was no longer in the best of health and not exactly companionable.

I poked her gently with my finger, and she opened bleary grey eyes and grinned, teeth like a row of worn black tombstones. "What is it, Lady Juliane? Are we in Normandy yet?"

Glumly, I shook my head. "Not even on the ship, Gundrada. There's a storm. Can you not hear the thunder?"

She cocked her head on one side in the manner of an inquisitive dog. "Now that you mention it, Lady...aye, I do. And there I thought it was my stomach grumbling." She prodded at the slack mound of her belly, which suddenly gave out an enormous gurgle.

"I do not know what is the best course to take—brave the sea or wait for a calm spell. The latter, I am told, may take months," I murmured as another distant blast of thunder reached my ears.

Gundrada reached over and patted my leg with a palsied claw. I tried not to cringe. "Don't you worry, my hen, though well I remember the eagerness of the young; no doubt you yearn for his embrace—as is natural in holy matrimony, for all the Church talks of sin!"

Agitated and a little embarrassed, I rolled my eyes. "It's not that at all, Gundrada. I've never even met this Eustace, let alone yearn for him. I am more afraid that if we press on, we will end up food for the fishes at the bottom of the sea! Yet at the same time, if we get stranded here...Well, does months stuck in Southampton appeal?"

Gundrada threw up her hands and cackled; I had no idea if she were truly amused by my words or if she was merely age-addled. Ignoring her, I stared at the canopy above, noting how it billowed in the gale and how its colour had grown darker as the rain began to lash...*It was leaking.* Droplets started to fall, wetting the quilts and furs. In misery, I groaned, drawing my one dry fur up around my ears. Gundrada continued to cackle as she tried to catch the water pouring through the top of the canopy in her cupped hands...

As it happened, the captain of our vessel decided to sail despite the weather. Darkness had fallen and the quay was alight with hundreds of lanthorn torches when we boarded the ship. Gundrada and I were hastily locked away in the hold; many sailors hated to go to sea with women aboard as they considered the presence of females unlucky, but as they were being paid in this instance from a King's purse, they kept their complaints to a minimum. Nonetheless, the captain clearly wanted me out of sight as quickly as possible. Quickness was also desirable because he wanted to be upon his way without further ado; he said he believed he could outrun the worst of the storm. He did not want to end up a prisoner of the English weather, since he wouldn't get paid a penny till his cargo reached Normandy safely.

The hold was dark and smelly, reeking of salt, dried meat and the livestock it had carried before us. The men of my entourage clustered in the darkness, seated with their weapons over their knees. Beyond them, a little booth had been set up for us women, hung around with draperies for privacy.

How kind, I thought cynically as I crawled behind the curtain and Gundrada scrambled after me, and we sat together in the dark on flat, musty pillows.

The lurching of the ship as it sped into the outer waters soon brought both of us to illness. After a short time, the spinning in my head had ceased, but Gundrada, who was supposedly there to bring comfort, lay groaning on my lap and spewing all over the salty boards. I held her grizzled head and prayed for a safe, swift journey to Normandy.

It was not a pleasant trip. Buffeted by the wind, the ship started rolling and bucking; items not fastened down securely were flung across the hold—a stool, a keg, a barrel of wine. We had to scramble aside to avoid injury. I saw my travelling chest skid away and the lid pop off, sending my garments flying about the hold. Cursing in an unladylike manner, I crawled after the box on hands and knees, stuffed my crumpled raiment back inside, then dragged it back to my little booth. "Here, Gundrada, lean on this," I told my maid, pointing to the chest.

The old woman moaned and attempted to sit; bile trickled from her nose and her eyes were watery and blood-red from all her heaving. My eyes watered too as the scent of vomit clawed at my nostrils. As gently as I could I propped Gundrada up against the chest; she flopped across the lid like a rag-doll, head lolling; gurgling noises continued to emerge from her throat.

All around was a tumult of water, the slap and bang of waves pounding on the hull as if demanding admittance; from a distance, over the sea's roar I heard the rumble of the thunder, deeper and more menacing than before, the bellows of hidden giants in the sky. I wondered what the sailors were doing on the deck above. Praying, most likely.

I decided I should add my prayers to theirs and hurriedly mumbled words to St Christopher, patron saint of travellers, followed by a rather appropriate passage from Exodus about the journey of the Israelites, "*The Lord went before them by day in a pillar of a cloud, to lead the way; and by night in a pillar of fire, to give them light…*"

After a while, though, my fear of being sucked into the deep dark maw of the sea quieted and exhaustion set in; I could barely keep my eyes open. Curled into a ball, I lay down beside Gundrada, and slowly, slowly as I drowsed, slipping in and out of proper sleep, the ship ceased to rock and the thunder stopped its fearsome booming.

When I awoke, feeling infinitely more cheerful, I forced myself to drink a mouthful of wine to fortify myself. The storm seemed to have blown itself out in the dark before dawn; the seas around us were quieter, making a rhythmic swishing against the prow of the ship. We would live!

"That wasn't so bad, Gundrada, was it?" I prodded the maid with the toe of my shoe.

Gundrada merely clutched her belly and retched yet again.

We arrived to find heavy rain falling over a gloomy port; it seemed Normandy's weather could be just as inclement as England's. I had tidied myself as best I could, putting on a neat wimple and changing my gown from my sweat-and-bile sodden travelling dress. I had no idea if my husband would be in the welcoming party but rather hoped he would be. At least I would have someone to converse with besides Gundrada; perhaps, on the journey to our home, I could even forge the beginnings of a harmonious marriage. Oh, I was under no illusion that this was ever going to be a love-match, but I desired the alliance to run as smoothly as possible.

But Eustace was not there, and the 'welcoming party' at the port was not, well, very welcoming—a cavalcade of dour Norman men in rusty mail and conical helmets who looked as if they longed to be anywhere but here. At least they had brought a large wheeled chariot for my use; quicker on the road, more comfortable than a litter and, hopefully, it would not leak.

Rain splashing about me, bouncing off the cobbles, I walked towards the chariot, legs still rather wobbly from our wild passage over the Narrow Sea. The day was failing, the light bluish and cold. None of the entourage made to help me up into the carriage. The water dragged my skirts down, making me slow and clumsy—I would look an ape if I clambered in, clothes and wimple askew, and I had no wish for these men—*my husband's men!*—to amuse themselves at my expense or perhaps even catch a glimpse of my bare legs.

"Will no one here hand a lady up?" I asked, my tone as cold as the rain sluicing down my neck.

A captain ambled over; big and broad, front teeth knocked out in some bygone brawl. "Milady, we are not courtiers," he said, his accent thick. I could barely understand him, although I had been taught Norman French from a young age at Mother's insistence. She was determined I should mingle easily with the elite and not overly favour the English tongue.

That you are not courtier is indeed clear, I thought angrily, looking the oafish soldier up and down, but I bit my treacherous tongue. It would not do to anger these men whose air seemed a mingling of diffidence and vague hostility. Curtly, I beckoned to Gundrada. "Help me, Gundrada, if you would. No one else is willing, it seems."

She hobbled over but she was so short and so weak from her bouts of seasickness, she was not much help. I had her hold out my cloak to keep me from public view and I managed to scramble into the chariot unaided. After, Gundrada folded the mantle up, and I dragged her inside like a sack of meal. At least no one laughed. I did not imagine any of these men laughed very often—unless it was while pillaging a town or killing an enemy.

Once settled inside, I yanked the draperies shut against the chill, the damp and the ugly visages of the soldiers beyond. The chariot began to judder down the rutted road; outside, harness and horse-bridles jingled with false merriness, while the rain, in a steady stream, hissed down.

As the journey progressed, a sense of doom overwhelmed me, tiredness and the strangeness of everything taking its toll; I felt like a lamb on its way to the slaughter. My mind whirled as I invented all sorts of terrible reasons why Eustace had not come to the port to greet his new wife—he was ill with plague, a priest at his bedside; he had a mistress he loved and had already decided to repudiate me; he was deformed and would not allow me to see his grotesqueness until I was locked behind the walls of his fortress and could not escape.

I sat bowed with misery, Gundrada huddled at my side, as the carriage rumbled on toward Jesu knows where.

My first view of Breteuil Castle was not an inspiring one. Bleak, dark, stocky, the keep with its tiny arrow-slits reared up like the head of an ugly giant, the conical turrets jabbing at the ever-weeping clouds. Rings stretched out across the muddy water of a square moat as raindrops slapped the surface with relentless ferocity.

Then the chariot was inside the walls and the gates closed with a loud metallic clang. The carriage trundled down the barbican and into the inner bailey where I could hear chickens squawking as they fluttered away from the heavy, slow-moving wheels. Scents of smoke, horses, animals and people wafted to my nostrils.

"I'm hungry," murmured Gundrada, rubbing her stomach. She seemed to be recovering from her ordeal at sea.

Our transportation came to a shuddering stop. I hesitated, not knowing if I should try to alight on my own or wait for help. I had no idea what men would consider gauche or improper in Normandy.

The door was jerked open and the concealing curtain twitched aside. My heart hammered, as a red, coarse face with a huge wen on the cheek butted through the hangings. No, I need not worry, it could not be Eustace—too old, old enough to be my husband's father.

"Who are you?" I asked, a little snappishly.

"Robert de Maine, my lord of Breteuil's chamberlain, my Lady," replied the man. "I am to take you to him." He held out his arm. His sleeve was poorly laundered, stained; his knuckles were hairy and his nails jagged. I forced myself not to look and took the proffered arm.

A moment later I was standing, blinking owlishly, in the rain-soaked bailey. Walls rose above me; men stalked them like beasts of prey, their spear butts crashing on stone, the sharp tips of their helms a row of fangs against the sky. Above them, on the watchtowers, were parties of archers, their bows bent as they gazed out across the lands beyond, scanning the horizon for enemies. Nearer to me, ankle-deep in mud churned up in the rain, stood the castle folk, the servants and locals who brought their wares to the castle to sell, manning the little rudely-thatched stalls covered that leaned against the inner curtain walls. They stared, not terribly politely, murmuring amongst themselves. I heard one laugh, braying like an ass, and froze, flushing.

"We must go. You are getting wet, milady," said Robert the Chamberlain. "It would not please the Lord Eustace to have his bride sick." He smiled at me, and though his smile was crooked, his teeth foul, at least there was a kind of vague warmth in his expression.

I hurried alongside him, grabbing up a bunch of my heavy skirts in one hand, Gundrada loping along on my heels, having managed to extricate herself from the chariot. She was grumbling under her breath and rolling her eyes like a madwoman.

The steps up the side of the keep were wooden and steep. Leading to the first-floor doorway with its rounded Romanesque arch, the wet slats gleamed dully in the light from two huge torches cinched above the entrance, sheltered from the downpour by a stone overhang bearing two goggle-eyed gargoyles. Fearful I might slip, I clutched the chamberlain's hefty arm and proceeded carefully along as the wind and rain buffeted me. Gundrada was almost on all fours like a dog; she cursed under her breath, a dismal noise full of anger and woe.

Then we were inside the castle. The wind dropped instantly and I was smitten by fug, the smell of old reeds and dog piss. Biting my lip in disgust, I followed the chamberlain down the corridor, up a wide flight of stairs and into the Hall where dozens of men—I could see no women—clustered at long benches. Frayed old banners were hanging from the beams and the rush-mats on the floor were scattered with old gnawed bones. It was clear where the rank scent that permeated the fortress was coming from.

The chamberlain halted, cleared his voice, then roared out, "The Lady Juliane FitzRoy, daughter of his Grace, King Henry of England."

The men seated at the tables halted their conversation and slammed down their chunky tankards. They were as rough-looking as those who had accompanied me to Breteuil, grizzled warriors in patchy boiled leather with their hair nigh shaven off. Clearly, this was a Norman backwater, filled with sellswords and men who lived only for war.

Head lifted high, I walked slowly down the centre of the hall after beckoning Gundrada to stay where she was. I approached the high table, where three men had risen in what I presumed was a greeting. This made it difficult, as I had no idea which one was Eustace de Breteuil. I supposed the tallest one, long-faced and black-haired, was too old, but both younger men were of similar age to myself. One had deep auburn hair, worn a little longer than the other men, and a narrow visage with sword-like nose and deep eyes. The third was a few inches shorter than the auburn-haired one, with short sandy curls and bushy brows—he was absently picking his nose as he observed me with cultivated disinterest.

Please, please, Lady Mary, Queen of Virgins...do not let the nose-picker be Eustace! I begged Our Lady.

At length, the reddish youth stirred. "My Lady, I bid you greetings this day. It is good for a man to have a wife, especially one so fair of visage and…" A grin split his face; his teeth shone as bright as white pearls, "of high and noble bloodline."

The men in the Great Hall released great roars of approval and banged their flagons on the trestle tables, making a hideous racket.

"I trust you are the Lord Eustace, my betrothed?" I asked, trying to mingle maidenly modesty with obvious curiosity.

"None other," he said. "At my side stands my tutor, Master Raymond de Grai, and my squire Geoffroi de Montmorency. I am sure you will come to know them well and see what loyal souls they are."

"I am sure, my lord," I murmured, not feeling so confident. Master Raymond raked me with a hard stare as if he thought I was an unfit distraction for his charge, while Geoffroi's piggy gaze drifted to something invisible near the ceiling, which was more of interest to him than his lord's new bride. All the while, the squire continued to impolitely prod his nose.

"Your quarters are waiting, Lady Juliane," said Eustace. "You must feel weary after such a long journey. You must rest so as to recover your strength as soon as possible, for it is my intent we finalise our marriage before much more time has passed. Not only is such a union a desirable thing, but it will consolidate my hold on Breteuil." A lusty glitter filled his eyes, making me blush, although I truly could not guess whether it was lust for me or for his lands.

"How…how soon?" I asked.

"Tomorrow," he said cheerfully, folding his arms. "The chaplain will wed us at the chapel within the donjon. Following that, there a great celebratory banquet shall take place…and once that is over, our union will be made 'perfect' as they say. A funny euphemism, isn't it, Geoffroi?" He glanced at Nose-Picker who finally ceased his uncouth digging and gave an affirmative grunt.

Suddenly Eustace leaned forward and impulsively kissed me on either cheek, making a loud smacking noise. "I am glad you have come. Lady Juliane. Your Father the King told me you were fair—he certainly did not lie. It is time I took a fitting wife and began to be treated as the lord I am—not a child. I can ride, I can fight—and in two years I will reach my full majority."

I had to speak out, the idea of rushing to wed and bed seemed preposterous. "I appreciate your ardour, my Lord Eustace…but tomorrow? The crossing to Normandy was a rough one, I have hardly had time…"

"Tomorrow it will be; I have told all my kin and allies to attend the marital festivities." His voice was firm and touched with a little sulkiness as if he had not appreciated my questioning his choices. "As I said, Lady Juliane, rest a while. You're not sickly, are you?"

On that rather unkind note, he turned away and began to converse with Geoffroi the oafish squire; now Nose-Picker was jigging about scratching his buttocks with his hand. The men in the hall returned to their noisy eating and drinking, the moment's distraction over.

I was clearly dismissed.

Robert the Chamberlain cleared his throat. "My Lady, if you step this way, I will show you your apartments."

My bedchamber and solar were not too unpleasant, although they had a cold, damp scent which signalled that they had lain unused for some time. I presumed Eustace's father's wife was either dead or had remarried; in any case, she had left the bed behind. It was big with a wooden headboard carved with scenes of the Annunciation. The faded yellow draperies, marred by a few dank splodges, were embroidered with leaping gazelles and unicorns.

I inspected the sheets; a little discoloured but they seemed reasonably clean. My biggest fear was that the former lady of Breteuil might have died on them…Not a pleasant though.

Gundrada was shuffling around, poking at the brazier which was, fortunately, filled with kindling, and unpacking my wooden chest, which a servant had hauled into the chamber. "I rather thought there would be more help, Lady," she grumbled.

"So did I," I admitted. "Did you notice…there are hardly any women here? Anywhere?"

"Breteuil is full of hard-bitten fighting men, Lady. Maybe even mercenaries." Gundrada began to smooth out a blue dress that Helie and Yvanne had doctored to fit me. My wedding dress—blue for Our Lady, a symbol of purity.

I felt a little tearful for a moment, standing in this cold foreign castle with an old woman in her dotage, my own mother miles away across the Narrow Sea, and a betrothed who seemed more interested in the chatter of his unappealing squire than me. Then steel entered my young soul and I blinked back any weak tears. I was a King's daughter and in no wise a coward. I would make this fortress my own; I would bring it beauty.

My deeds here would become so famous they would spread throughout the whole of Europe. *Lady Juliane de Breteuil*, they would say, *none shall ever forget her…*

At dawn the next day, as streaks of rosy red light crept through gaps in the shutters, I rose from my bed, trembling in the cold, barefoot and dishevelled. Climbing from her straw-stuffed pallet, Gundrada helped me into my blue wedding gown and combed out my hair until it gleamed like a raven's wing. I ran my fingers through its length, drawing its coils forward over my shoulder; this was the last day I would be able to walk out with it uncovered.

Shortly after, a squire arrived—mercifully, not Geoffroi Nose-Picker, but a weedy lad of about fourteen summers—and he guided me, a torch clutched in one fist, to the castle chapel on the upper floor of the great keep. I was to arrive before Eustace, for my royal descent gave me precedence.

The chapel was small and old, its chancel arch pecked out with surreal beaked monsters and thorny-spined dragons. Inside the nave, the censers chugged out heady smoke in a forest of stout, umber-striped pillars,

I paused before the door, demure, waiting, although my innards churned—what if my groom had changed his mind and would leave me standing there alone, foolish in my sky-hued gown? But no, he could not; the agreement had been made in our absence, the *verba de presenti* spoken by Father's ambassadors on my behalf—Eustace and I were legally already married, although our union was as yet unconsummated.

Footsteps sounded in the corridor. Out of the corner of my eye, I saw Eustace approach, dressed in his best—fine leather shoes, an amber-coloured silk tunic imported from the exotic East, a rich red mantle trimmed with squirrel fur. His tutor Raymond de Grai was beside him, and annoying Geoffroi, wearing gaudy parti-colour that made me think of a court Fool, and behind them were men I did not know, dressed richly—I presumed the lords who would aid Eustace to administer Breteuil and its lands until he reached his majority.

Eustace gave me a small smile and my heart stirred a little. He was not so unattractive, certainly preferable to any of the village lads who had sniffed around Mother's home, where they were chased away with derision—I was a bastard but a royal one; they could only dream of marrying a maiden of such standing.

Upright, head held high, Eustace took his place at my side. A silver band held his reddish waving hair away from his brow. The sun, streaming through a narrow window one of the servants had unshuttered to give additional light, turned his locks to flame.

A thin priest, tall but bent like a sickle, with a pock-marked right cheek and hair like wisps of grey smoke, emerged from the gloomy corridor. Bible in hand, he stood before us outside the entrance to God's House as was appropriate for a rite that was blessed in the eyes of Mother Church but yet not one of the sacraments.

He eyed Eustace and I, asking questions that would have seemed impertinent if they were not traditional and necessary—"Are you both of age?' "Did you receive the permission of your parents to marry?" "Are you related within the prohibited degree?"

When he was satisfied that we had given true answers, he read aloud before all gathered there the terms of my dowry. Father had provided money, plate, and, of course, lands. I thought it was a very generous amount but as the list of lands and castles was read out, I saw Eustace scowl—but only for a moment. Next minute he was back to himself, serious and intent on the priest's word. I was uneasy; did he not think the King had fulfilled all obligations with this dowry? If it were so, his belief was outrageous! Although Eustace and I were both bastards, through my womb Eustace's children would be born of the stock of Kings!

I tried to put thoughts of my husband's possible ingratitude away from my mind and concentrated on the priest and the holy words he mumbled, his thick, unfamiliar dialect making him hard to follow. Beyond all hope, I managed to make the correct replies in an audible voice that did not waver or break, and before I knew it, Eustace was placing a plain gold wedding band upon the third finger of my right hand. He struggled to get it past my knuckle and for a moment I feared it was too small, but he persisted in his quest, and eventually it slid into place, a little tight but not unbearable. From this day on, it would never leave my finger…

A bag of coins was thrust into my hand by the castle Treasurer; these were for distribution to the poor later in the day. Then the priest started welcoming the members of the assembly into the confines of the chapel and Eustace and I were placed beneath a cloth canopy and a Mass was said. Once done, the priest gave my new husband the kiss of peace, and Eustace turned to me and gave me the same kiss in turn.

As his lips pressed on mine, a strange, alien sensation, an unfamiliar warmth flooded my body—but it was followed by a sharp shiver of fear. I was his, he was mine, for good or for ill, forever and ever.

The wedding feast ran long into the night. Eustace's ruffians drank and belched and farted while ripping like ravenous beasts into plates of pork and venison. One oaf even slapped another with an eel slathered in saffron sauce, and all who witnessed this foolery thought it a great source of mirth. Gundrada was near enough the only woman there other than me; she hovered around my seat, whining nervously under her breath, looking disconcerted and out of place. As I did.

"Peace," I said quietly to her as she attended me on the high dais, helping adjust my robes and cutting up my food where necessary. "I swear it will not be like this always. I will see changes made now that I am Countess. I swear it…"

"Ooh, Lady Juliane," Gundrada croaked. "I do hope you are right. One of those churls said I looked a right witch and deserved to be dragged to the ducking stool."

"Don't listen to such nonsense; it's born of drink. I assure you this behaviour will change now that I am lady of the household."

Someone coughed softly at my shoulder. I jumped. It was Eustace's tutor, Raymond de Grai. "My Lady Countess, if I may speak…"

I nodded, beckoning him closer.

"I am guessing your ladyship finds this place…crude, a haven of rough men."

My cheeks burned; he must have overheard my conversation with Gundrada. Was I that loud and indiscreet? Or was I being watched?

"There is a reason the Lord Eustace has surrounded himself with such men. As you know, he was born a bastard. When his sire, the Lord William died, many of his kin tried to stake a claim on Breteuil. Chief amongst them was his uncle William de Gael of Brittany—his mother, Emma, was old Lord William's sister. Reginald de Grancey also made a rival claim. They were rejected by the local barons but they have not forgotten Breteuil. They would wrest the castle and its lands from such a young, untried lordling's hands had they the chance. So Eustace has surrounded himself by mercenaries as protection. I advised him against it, but he was insistant."

My breath caught in my throat. "Are there any men of good worth who will support my husband should it come to it? Men who would fight for honour and loyalty—not money?"

Master Raymond nodded. "Ralph Rufus of Pont Echanfray—see, the red-haired man in the fine cloak? He is one. William Aliz, with the long black beard—he is another. You might find Arnold du Bois and Roger de Glos will stand behind Lord Eustace solidly, and perhaps the Fresnel family."

"My Father the King of England will support him too," I said stalwartly, although I truly did not know my sire's mind. I knew Henry had given support to Eustace in his claim and wedding me to him was a further seal of approval. Breteuil and Pacy were prominent areas of the Duchy and he needed allies since his dealings with the Duke of Normandy, his brother Robert, were frequently acrimonious. But if it came down to swords and arrows—who knew? He had other important business elsewhere.

"I am sure of it, Countess." The man bowed, smiling in what I thought was a slightly supercilious fashion. "At least you know now why this castle is not a pleasure palace filled with music and flowers and dancing maidens. There have also been no females here since Lord Eustace's sisters were wed and the former Countess of Breteuil passed into the keeping of God."

"I understand," I said, but in my mind I thought, *That may be, but it must change; still I will make this place anew if I can....*

The marriage feast was over. I was escorted by a pair of pages to the bridal chamber where Gundrada divested me of my festive clothes with trembling fingers. "Oh, oh, I cannot go fast enough!" she moaned as we both heard the sound of my groom and his band of revellers mounting the stairs, whooping and yelling over the music played by accompanying musicians.

"Take your time, Gundrada," I said firmly. "The bolt is on the door; we will not permit them entrance till I am ready."

Will I ever truly be ready for this? I thought with sudden fearfulness. Oh, I was no brainless, innocent ninny; I'd grown up in the country and had seen bulls mate with cows and once, yes, a servant girl and a stable-boy rolling in the hay. I'd thought the wench was hurt at first, with her shrieks and groans, but when I, a child of ten hiding in the loft to avoid a beating owed for disrespecting Mama, had angled to see the girl's face, I noticed her expression was certainly not one of pain, and so I put away the pewter pot I'd thought of hurling at her 'attacker's' head.

But this was different. It was *me*, for one. And I was far from my mother's guidance, although one might not think a King's concubine a good guide in marital bliss anyway, at least not in the teaching of morality. My heart started to hammer and my head whirled; I took deep breaths and tried to calm myself.

Gundrada had released all the ties on my clothes and I stood naked and cold in the chamber. She took a bowl of scented water standing on the table and began to lave me with it from head to toe. Then with one tremulous hand, she drew back the coverlet on the bed; below, hundreds of dried rose petals lay strewn, giving off a sweet, almost sickly scent.

"In you go, my Lady," she said. "I can hear those ruffians…I mean your husband the Lord Eustace and his companions, nigh on pounding at the door."

My black hair swinging, falling over me like a raven cloak, I slipped between the bed-sheets, drawing the coverlet up to my shoulders.

Outside the door there were hoots and bawdy singing:
There was a young lord of great renown,
A young lord who came riding down,
And he did swive a girl from town!

He took her out behind the mill,
He took her out to get his fill,

And, he did swive her up the hill!

He took her to his bachelor's bed,
He took her till the night was fled,
And, he did swive her till she was dead!

And when the bells rang out "Amen,"
And when the bells rang out "Now then!"
He did swive her back to life again!

And now the moral I will tell,
When all the world seems bleak and fell,
Go and swive 'till all be well!

Gundrada hobbled to the door and pulled back the piece of wood barring it. The door swung inwards with a loud bang, making Gundrada stagger back and almost fall to the floor. More enraged than embarrassed or afraid, she began to hurl imprecations at the incomers, but no one could hear her curses in the cacophony of blaring instruments and bellowing men.

Into the bridal chamber they swaggered, a pile of lords all drunk and crimson-faced. In the middle was my inebriated husband, head lolling, hair mussed as they held him up to keep him from falling. The other nobles taunted him and made crude gestures as they began to pull off his drink-stained garments. Every now and then, they glanced toward me with hot, eager eyes, no doubt hoping the coverlet I clutched to my breast would somehow slip or become transparent.

As Eustace's fine woollen hose was flung across the room, I averted my eyes modestly as befitting a maiden, which brought another volley of gleeful shouts from the wedding party.

As he was dragged to the bed and hurled upon it, he writhed in embarrassment, tried vainly to cover himself, and shouted, his voice slurred, "Out of here now, you lot…all of you. I have had enough!"

"You haven't had any yet!" a moustached man in a green cap roared, and the others fell laughing around the chamber, drunkenly crashing into the furniture, upending the ewer for ablutions and tripping over the huddled, disapproving form of Gundrada, who showing mettle I had not known she possessed, spat at them like an affronted cat.

The men only began to file out of the bedchamber when the priest arrived to give the customary blessing of the bed. As they marched away down the halls, chanting and singing ribald verse, the priest entered the room and glanced around, although I had no doubt he had seen it several times before—he was no youngster and had likely even witnessed Eustace's birth. His rheumy gaze found Gundrada; she hoisted her rumpled skirts with a disgusted sniff and shuffled from the room, although I had no doubt she'd linger nearby, far from the sotted revellers.

"Bless, O Lord, this sleeping chamber," the priest intoned, standing before the great bed where Eustace lay sprawled sideways like a fish out of water, trying vainly to gather some dignity in his drunk and naked condition. "You who watches over Israel, watch over thy servants who rest in this bed. Guard them against fantasies and the illusions of devils, guard them in waking, guard them in slumber, and here, there and everywhere that they may need your protection."

Then he approached the side of the bed. Eustace managed to roll in beside me; I jumped as I felt the hot touch of his outer thigh against mine.

"Let us pray," said the priest, making the sign of the cross. "God bless your bodies and souls as he blessed those of Abraham, Isaac and Jacob. May the Lord send his holy angel to guard and tend you all the long days of your lives. The Father, the Son and the Holy Ghost bless you, triune in number, and One in name. Amen."

Words spoken, he sprinkled Holy Water upon us and upon the petal-strewn sheets before departing in a rustle of vestments. The door closed.

My husband and I were alone. Clumsily he began to stroke my unbound hair. "You need not be afraid, Juliane," he slurred.

"I am not afraid," I said. It was not strictly true but I would not reveal that to him. I was in a new country, beginning a new, unfamiliar life; to show fear would be to show weakness. I guessed very much that weakness in anyone, even a woman, might not prove a good thing in this unsettled part of Normandy.

"Oh?" He leaned on one elbow, eyes bleary.

"Why would I be? You have sworn this day to love and honour me."

"It often does not end up so."

I raised my brows. "What shall I say then, husband? That if you do harm me, my father the King of England should kill you?"

"He might and all." Eustace suddenly laughed. "Ah, he has been good to me, His Highness King Henry. I have much to be grateful for—his support of my claim to Breteuil."

"And his eldest daughter, even though baseborn," I said, with a teasing smile.

"Yes, that too. That most of all…" Abruptly, he grasped my shoulders, drawing me towards him. His mouth burned on mine, tasting of the spices in the wine he had drunk. "I like you, wife. I think we shall be…good together."

I pulled my lips from his but let his hands linger where they would. I was his now…but there was a little matter to resolve. "On this night of all nights," I whispered in his ear as he trailed small, drunken kisses down my neck, my breasts, my belly, "I ask you to grant me one wish."

"If I can, I will," he murmured, lifting the dark curtain of my hair, revealing my pale, shining nakedness. Flecks of Holy Water still glimmered on my skin; the sight seemed to increase his ardour and his breath came out in a gasp. "Speak on, Juliane."

"This castle—it sore needs a woman's touch."

"And so you are here."

"I appreciate that your hold on Breteuil has been contested by many—but the castle needs a garden to walk and grow herbs in, it needs the privies flushed out and it needs the hall scoured and those rushes burnt. And…it is not some border fortress, full of reivers. I would not suffer roistering lords every night. I will have musicians and troubadours of my choice. And women."

"Women?"

"Yes, women. Ladies-in-waiting to attend to my needs. To be companions when you are away. To help me oversee the running of your household."

"You have that…that old crone from England, don't you?"

I gave him a frustrated look. "As you say, she is ancient. The King sent her because she's a childless widow, more loyal than most knights, but also not much use anymore. Truth be told, it is time she was put to pasture, like a noble horse. She should be pensioned off, Eustace, and younger women brought in."

He frowned. "The girls in the town are slovenly…and sluts," he said.

And how do you know that? I narrowed my eyes in annoyance but continued. "God's Teeth, Eustace, I don't mean peasant girls; that would hardly be fitting, would it? No, some of the barons in neighbouring lands must have daughters who would gladly serve in our household."

"I will see."

"Good…and the rest of it?"

"I will see about that too. You…you are most likely right. The castle was not as it was in my Father's day. Nothing has been the same since…Juliane, do you know what happened to him?"

Blankly I shook my head.

A pained expression crossed my husband's face. "He was captured by Ascelin Gouel de Percival, the Wolf, and tortured in his dungeons."

I gasped in dismay. "How vile! What cause did this lord have to harm him?"

"Lord Ascelin desired my sister Isabella to wife. The match was not agreeable to my sire and he told him no. The Wolf then laid in wait for him in the woods—just like the ravening beast he is named for. He took hold of him, beat him, then dragged him to his stronghold where he bound him in chains. He said he would not let my Father free until he agreed to let him marry Isabella. In the end, under duress, he said yes to Ascelin. He had no choice—it was that or starve in the dungeon."

"Was this Wolf enamoured of the lady so much he could find no other?"

Eustace laughed harshly. "My sister is fair enough, no doubt about it…but Father had agreed to split our inheritance between us. He was very fond of Isabella. I am sure money and lands attracted Ascelin Gouel more than Isabella's beauty."

He frowned, drawing away from me and clutching the covers around him. "Father was a fool to have left castles and lands to a woman. He did not do it with my other sister, Isabel, who has a different mother. Trouble was bound to come of it. The ravening Wolf took the Castle of Ivry—which should have been part of my inheritance, not Isabella's."

"Oh, what a shame…" I tried to soothe him; I did not understand these desires for a constant stream of new castles—they were expensive to maintain and a source of trouble. "Could nothing be done by Duke Robert?"

"He forced Ascelin and Isabella out…but the castle did not go to me as it should have done. Duke Robert holds it now and has installed his own castellan there. I *liked* that castle; it is very mighty—and…and by all that is right and proper, it should be mine!"

I did not like this turn in his mood. A shadow lay over him and there was a fierceness in his manner I had not noted before. "Maybe one day it shall be," I soothed, sliding my arms around him from behind, pressing my bare flesh to his.

He forgot his woes over castles and manors. He whipped around and flung himself atop me with a passion that seemed almost angry. "I will have Ivry, Juliane—I swear it," he said.

"Let's not talk more about lands," I said. "I am sorry for your Father's plight."

"He is dead now, and he was weak. And yes, let us turn our attention from idle talk to greater pleasures." He pressed me down into the bed linens. He was my age yet seemed older, more experienced—well, what had I expected, these Norman boys learned young!

"So…you will not forget to seek me out some ladies-in-waiting soon, Eustace?" I needed an answer.

"Yes, yes, anything to keep you happy, wife."

I spoke no more and drew him down to me, following his movements, tentatively touching his bare flesh. He said he would keep me happy—now was my turn to make *him* happy in any way I could.

CHAPTER THREE

I soon settled into my new life as the wife of the Count of Breteuil. As requested, three maidens were enlisted from amongst the families of local knights and barons to attend me as my ladies-in-waiting. They were my age, one blonde, two brunette, all giggly and fun-living, interested in music and dance and womanly arts. Their names were Heloise, Cecelie and Idonea.

Poor old Gundrada was greatly put out at first, thinking she was being thrust aside—which, in truth, she was. I calmed her with kindly words, saying that I feared for her health if she continued to serve me without assistance. I even offered to send her back to England, if she wished—which made my Lord Husband's face shrivel in annoyance, for the purse strings were still held by his guardians and he had to ask permission for any expenditure. I assured him my father would pay Gundrada's way home but as it happened, she chose to stay at Breteuil Castle, where she was given her own little room near the vast kitchens and spent most of the day snoring in front of the fire-brazier.

The tiring-maidens picked out, I then became acquainted with the castle staff—and hired many more from the village. I gave orders for the castle to be cleaned from turret to cellar and I gave the pantler instructions for obtaining fresher and less stodgy food—more fish, less beef and pork—and told cook exactly how I wanted it served.

There were fewer gatherings of knights in the hall and less consumption of ale, beer and wine. I heard some of the local thugs, scarce more than robber-barons in my estimation, saying that Eustace was crushed 'beneath my thumb' but I cared nothing for their disrespect—I was just glad they were no longer loitering about the castle like the smell of an uncleaned privy. Oh, I had *that* problem dealt with too; a gong-farmer raked the dung out of the clogged vents at the edge of the moat while I ordered the odious Geoffroi to round up the other squires and help sluice down the privy shutes from the top. He whined the whole time, running red-faced up and down the stone steps with tubs of water from the well, while Cecelie, Idonea, and Heloise hung about watching, holding posies of flowers over their noses to cut the smell.

I worried if Eustace might not find pleasure in the new ideas I brought—but it seemed he did or at least pretended so. Geoffroi was no longer his closest companion; he banished him to dwell with the other squires, and eventually Nose-Picker left Breteuil to contaminate another noble household. With my guidance, Eustace began to take delight in more refined pastimes—things we could enjoy together—games of chess upon a lovely chessboard of polished black and white stone that had come as part of my dowry; boating on the lake below Castle Hill; hunting with hounds in the nearby forest; hawking with a pair of gyrfalcons which I purchased for him. Oh, and making love, of course, in our bed with new curtains broidered with lions to remind him of my ancestry. We found ourselves rather well-matched in that way, if not so much in some others, and I was determined he, unlike my sire, would not have twenty or more bastards running about the countryside!

By the time he came to his majority at eighteen, I was pregnant, my belly big and round beneath my gowns. I was uncomfortable and calling curses on Mother Eve in private, while my husband strutted about the castle like a proud peacock, acting if he were the only man that had ever fathered a babe.

A month before the child was born, I wrote my will as all sensible noblewomen did, for it was often the case that the woman did not survive the birth. The thought made me unhappy with a female's lot and I was short with Eustace, who seemed unaware of the risk to me and spent time bragging about the son he would soon have, the lawful, legal son who would live a grand life with none of the problems a bastard such as Eustace had faced.

"You had best pray on your knees that I survive," I said nastily, my ankles swollen like an old woman with dropsy, my back feeling as if it would snap in two. "It would go ill for you I would imagine if you didn't have my father's support against the rapacious wolves around here—the kind who walk on two legs. The men you supplanted, who thought they had a legitimate claim, are still just biding their time, I'd wager."

"I know," he said, calmer than I thought he'd be, "and you're not going to die. Do not say such things—it brings ill-luck."

"So you imagine yourself God now, who sees all things and knows the outcome," I snapped, pressing my hands to my aching back. "You're a heathen."

"No, I merely despise such melancholy thoughts, which are useless. Hah, if you die, I'll just have to ask King Henry if he has another bastard daughter I can marry…I'm sure he had plenty!"

I threw an orange at him from the gilded bowl on the table; immediately regretted it, for it was imported and the last one we had, and since I fell with child, I had craved sweet oranges.

Eustace walked out of the room, clutching the orange, which he had caught neatly in his hand. Slowly he peeled it—for himself. I wished I had something else to throw.

My confinement was dull, as I had guessed it would be. Window shutters were kept closed and the fires were stoked although it was not particularly cold. There was plenty to eat, a renowned midwife, and all my ladies-in-waiting, including Gundrada, who insisted she had a few midwifery skills herself, but the chamber was too dim and airless, and eventually smelly from the scent of two many bodies kept close in the warm. Even the posies of flowers Heloise scattered in abundance did little good to freshen the place.

My temper was worse than ever. I made Cecelie sing for me as she had a pleasant voice. Heloise read passages from my missal. Lots of sewing and chattering went on—to the point I thought my head would burst from frivolous nonsense or that I might grab the sewing-needle and stab someone.

And then the pains came, washing over me in cramping waves…My child was coming and all that birth entailed. Ill-temper changed to fear

But for me, unlike so many women, the birth of my first babe turned out to be surprisingly easy, even though I had heard the terrible tales of travail that lasted days. My pangs started at sundown and by dawn the next morning, I was delivered of a baby son with a lusty set of lungs.

"You have wide child-bearing hips, my Lady," Gundrada said to me, her whiskery chin all a-tremble with the joy of my safe delivery. "I hope you don't mind me saying so."

I did mind a little because her 'compliment' made me sound a great carthorse, but it would have seemed petulant to complain about such a triviality on such a joyous morn. I had delivered, I had done my duty and both my child and I were alive.

Eustace was elated. "I knew it would be a boy!" he cried, dandling the baby once he was nicely cleaned-up and swaddled. "Juliane, you are the best wife a man could have. I will give you anything you desire. Name it."

I lay back in my bed, exhausted but triumphant, thinking on his words. "You know…when I am strong again, and when I have been properly churched, I would like a little journey away from Breteuil." I remembered old promises made in England—now was the time to keep them.

"Away from Breteuil?" He eyed me nervously; I suspected he thought I was about to ask for a trip to see my mother. I would have loved to, but I was aware that would prove far too costly. However, I had other kin in Normandy.

"My half-sister Matilda is married to the Count of Perche, as you know. Would it not be sisterly for us to meet up? I have heard she has two infant daughters, Philippa and Felicia. Maybe one of them might prove suitable, in the future, for our son, making a strong alliance with Perche. Yes, they are related within the forbidden degrees, but there is really no reason why the Pope would not grant a dispensation for a marriage between one of them and our…our…What are we going to call him?"

"William," said Eustace firmly. "After my father."

I frowned; I always thought William of Breteuil had sounded a rather weak and unprepossessing man and Eustace had never shown any sign of holding him in high esteem ere now. However, tradition held sway—and William was a name I favoured myself.

"Yes, I like that," I said, staring down at the baby's sleeping face. "After your sire, and my esteemed grandfather, the Duke of Normandy—the Conqueror," I added.

William it was.

The following spring, Eustace gave into my wishes and we journeyed to Perche to meet with Tilda and her husband, Count Rotrou. I was with child again and my husband tried to dissuade me from travelling the long miles, especially as there had been some unrest amongst the nobles of Normandy—Duke Robert, my uncle, ever fractious and envious of Henry's crown, the notorious sadist Robert de Belleme, exiled from England, and fiery William of Mortain being prime instigators, but I had my heart set on seeing my sister and felt fine besides, being early into my pregnancy and not yet afflicted by the worst of its discomforts. It was hard to leave little Will behind in the nursery but Gundrada was clucking over him like a watchful hen, and he had a plump wetnurse called Aude, and a gaggle of other nursemaids to see to his needs.

From my curtained litter, I managed to watch the world go by; endless villages, endless fields and trees, cows and peasants, goats and herders, geese and goose-girls, a man rolling a vast wheel of cheese that bounced along the track like a glowing but ill-smelling sun…

At last, we reached the Perche, and the castle of the Counts, towering high over the Huisne Valley. It was a great grim block with a ring of towers encircling it.

Eustace, riding alongside the outer curtain wall, seemed to like it. "A fine fortress," he said, a hint of envy in his voice. "It reminds me of Ivry."

Ivry. I bit my lip in frustration. He was always on about the ownership of that castle—an unhealthy fixation, but his acquisitiveness was one that all high-born Normans seemed to have. I could say that without insult, having Norman blood too, mingling with that of the Saxon.

Tilda came to greet us in the Great Hall, which was very great indeed, with a high, vaulted ceiling painted with angels and stars. Behind her, a pair of nurses carried her two little children, Philippa and Felicia, the youngest just a few months old, the elder almost two. She had been conceived on Tilda's wedding night. Both children were fair-cheeked and golden-haired like their mother.

"Sister," I embraced her. "It is good to see you after so long."

"And you made good your promise that you would come." Tilda twined her fingers with mine. "I am so glad. How have you fared these past years?"

"I am a mother even as you—to a son called William. And breeding again." I touched my belly, barely showing under my thick robes.

"A son, how marvellous," she sighed. "I have not been fortunate enough to give my lord his heir—yet."

Standing near my shoulder, Eustace looked uncomfortable at all this talk of womanish things. He jigged about in his long travelling cloak, holding out his hands to the fire-pit to get the warmth after our long ride. "And where, Countess Matilda, is the great Lord Rotrou? Surely he has not forgotten the Count of Breteuil was coming to call?"

Tilda gave my husband her sweetest smile. "Of course, he has not forgotten, my lord—but you must understand my husband is an active man who, even in times of peace and with a happy household, cannot bear to warm his feet by the fire and drowse. This morning the verderers and foresters reports of a huge wild boar in the nearby woods, and so he has taken his men and gone on the hunt."

She had no sooner spoken than the door on the right side of the hall banged open and in stormed a robust man, marked as the Count by the coat of arms upon his tabard—white with red chevrons sharp as spearheads. The chevron's redness was rather muted, however, for Rotrou was covered in blood from head to toe. He wore a mail coif and the blood was even embedded in its links; it was also smeared all over his face—a broad, sun-tanned face with a long moustache that was, at the moment, painted with gore.

For brief seconds we all stared at each other in shock. The nurses carrying Tilda's babes cried out and smuggled their small charges away, even as the elder, Philippa, began to howl in fear. They were far too young to understand the gory pleasures of noblemen.

Eustace looked the blood-soaked Count up and down with what I could only guess was a spot of envy. "So, my Lord of Perche, it was a good hunt then?"

The Count stared back and suddenly gave a bellow of mirth. "You must be Eustace of Breteuil. You have arrived earlier than I expected. And yes, yes, the hunt was most exhilarating…" Turning on his heel, which was also caked with mud and guts, he snapped his fingers loudly in the direction of the corridor leading to the Hall.

In processed his huntsmen, bearing, tied to a pole by its feet, the most terrifying creature I had ever seen—a huge dead boar, with bristles sharp as blades and twisted tusks stained with crimson. The men dropped the carcass on the floor before Lord Rotrou; it made a massive thud and flecks of congealed blood flew, making a crimson pattern all over Tilda's pale green skirts. I thought she might shriek in disgust but instead, rather like a patient Madonna, she merely tilted her head on high and stared up in silence at the paintings on the ceiling.

"Heh, he is magnificent, is he not?" Rotrou leaned over to manipulate the boar's head with its gaping jaws lined by pink froth. I shuddered.

Eustace looked amazed and more openly envious. I could tell he wished the Count had wait and taken him on his hunt. He'd never taken down anything fiercer than a deer at Breteuil. "He is…he is a beauty!" he stammered.

"Beauty? As ugly as a troll, I'd say!" laughed Rotrou, letting the boar's head drop with a thud. The great curved tusks scored the rush mats. "But I'll wager the beast will make a fine centrepiece for a banquet!"

And so he did. Cooked in the spacious kitchens of the castle, the boar was served up to us the next day on a huge silver platter, his head still on, his capacious jaws stuffed with candied fruits. Alongside the boar, we were given choices of pheasant and woodcocks, eels and pike. Broth simmered in thick trenchers made of the finest white bread, and fritters, crepes and tarts sweetened by honey and almond milk were temptingly on hand.

I gazed out of the corner of my eye at our host, Count Rotrou. He was, thankfully, cleaner than yesterday, dressed in a floor-length saffron robe with a sturdy belt girding his midriff. His hair was cropped short in Norman style and was rather spikey; a dark brown colour, it held streaks of premature grey. His face was cheerful, his moustache long, his eyes a watery grey-green. He was not as old as I had expected from Tilda's words back in England—perhaps he was ten to twelve years her senior, but certainly no greybeard in his dotage—rather, a strong man in his prime.

As he bawled for more wine and devoured his hard-won boar, belching and burping and making Tilda shrink in weary embarrassment with trumpets from his buttocks, he seemed the rough, rude kind of man I had endeavoured to eject from Eustace's company—but I knew the Count of Perche was far more than just an oaf handy in battle with his sword. He had done much good for Perche and the people of the region called him 'the Great'—besides that, he had done God's work and fared on the First Crusade with Uncle Robert. Later, in thanksgiving for his safe return, he had even asked to become a confrater of the Abbey of Cluny. He had granted money to the monks by charter and laid the palm taken from holy Jerusalem upon their altar.

"So…tell me about your adventures in the Holy Land," said Eustace, staring at him, fascinated. Like most young men, he dreamed of Crusade, of seeing the mysterious lands of the east and routing the infidel.

Rotrou needed no prompting. Clearing his throat, he got to his feet, goblet clutched in his hand. "I…I was at the Siege of Antioch, my friend. My commander was the great Bohemond of Taranto—a worthy prince! You should have seen Antioch, Count Eustace—no common castle, that! Four hundred towers studded its walls. Four hundred!"

Eustace murmured his wonderment.

"And that is not all! For all its vast walls, sweeping away for miles, there were only six gates, three in the north wall, one in the west, one in the east and one in the south. All bristling with the paynim foe. And above all, separate from the city was the Citadel, built high above on the pinnacle of Mount Silpius. The place looked impregnable; we were all struck with awe at the sight of it. We also knew a siege might take many months, which it did, and that heathen forces from beyond might seek to come down on us like the hammer on the anvil, crushing us between their infantry and the defenders of the city walls."

"Antioch was once a Byzantine city, was it not?" I asked. "Did not many Christians still dwell there when you arrived, although paying fines to their Paynim overlords?"

Rotrou turned to me in surprise, his green-grey eyes blinking. He blinked frequently—he said his eyes had been burnt by the hot sun of the Holy Land, making them water constantly. "Ah, a lady of learning!" he bellowed. "How unusual! My dearest Matilda is interested in only the gentle arts such as sewing and dancing."

Tilda forced a little smile and stared down into her lap, ever the doting, submissive Norman wife.

I leant over the table toward Rotrou. "My Lord, I had no choice but to learn…I am a *terrible* dancer."

Rotrou burst out into loud laughter but as quick as it had come, his mirthfulness passed and his visage darkened. "I will tell you more of the tale, Countess Juliane, Count Eustace. The Governor of Antioch was a Moslem called Yaghi-Siyan. When he heard of the Christian army's approach, he took vengeance on the Christians who had been in his care. He herded up all those of note and drove them out of the gates. He imprisoned John the Oxite, the Patriarch of Antioch, in a foul dungeon. Worst of all, he turned St Paul's Cathedral into a stable for his cavalrymen's steeds!"

A mutter of shock passed around the chamber; men and women crossed themselves at hearing of such an outrage. The household had doubtless heard the tale many times before—yet still feelings ran high at the imagining of such desecration in God's House.

Count Rotrou's face became solemn beneath the drooping handle of his moustache; he knew he had an audience now. "With that evil deed accomplished and stallions eating hay from the high altar while their shite dappled the cathedral floors, Yaghi-Siyan then sent messages to his allies, asking for reinforcements. Sure enough, they came, marching across the dry and hostile terrain—leaders with names such as Duqaq, Toghtekin, Kerbogha…"

The gathered assembly gasped in horror, shaking their heads at the sound of those outlandish Saracen names. Surely those guttural monikers were fit only for demons from Hell!

Rotrou continued, his eyes burning as he remembered the battles he had fought: "We fought our way across the Iron Bridge, and with Lord Bohemond camped beside St Paul's Gate and there laid siege to the city. It was to be a long siege and a bitter one, I tell you—from the start we were bombarded with many missiles from the walls; they fell day and night and gave us no peace. Eventually, we had to build an earthen fort called Malregard to protect ourselves.

"By the time winter came, we were as starved as the inhabitants of Antioch—perhaps even more so. Bohemond led us on a foraging mission—we aimed to steal a flock of sheep—but out of the gloom rode Duqaq of Damascus and his warriors. We beat him off but many of our party were injured—and we had lost our precious flock. We returned to the camp, despairing, only to be terrified by a great rumbling and shaking of the earth that sent our horses mad. Many thought God had abandoned us, showed us signs of his displeasure."

"And still you remained, " said Eustace, as entranced as a little boy listening to childhood tales of knights in battle.

"Aye. Bohemond had heard that Kerbogha was coming with his army so he was forced to make a move. He had made contact with an Armenian inside the city called Firouz, and a deal was struck." Rotrou made a motion with his fingers to indicate the counting of coins. "Firouz was the guard of the Tower of the Two Sisters. He told us to scale the Tower when he was on his watch. Under the cover of darkness, a small party of us scaled the height of that great building— I was one of them, one of the first three soldiers of God to set foot in Antioch!"

Cheering sounded throughout the Great Hall. The minstrels began to play and a jongleur bawled out a song praising Count Rotrou's courage and prowess. A couple of tumblers began their gymnastics around the burning firepit, their lithe bodies silhouetted against the flames.

"Do you not want to hear the rest?" Rotrou's voice was lost in the cacophony of sound.

It seemed no one did. They had doubtless heard it all before, dozens of times. I turned my attention to my trencher, fearing an explosion of anger but Rotrou merely grinned and beckoned to a squire to refill his goblet. "To friendship…and alliance," he said to Eustace and the two of them clashed their jewelled cups together.

In the morning, my husband and the Count of Perche went riding together. I wandered the castle gardens with Tilda. She looked a little weary and mournful. "You are happy, sister?" I asked.

"I accept what I am given," she said.

Not good, I thought.

"What is wrong?" I laid my fingers on her arm.

Suddenly her eyes filled with tears. "Did you not see my littlest, Felicia? She is weak and ailing. I fear she will not live to see adulthood. My travail was hard with Philippa, I bled much—but Rotrou is a…a lusty man and he would not keep from my bed as soon as it was acceptable to the Church for him to enter it." A bitter expression crossed her face. "He had no care that the midwives thought more time was needed. I do not know why he was so insistent—it is not as if he does not have mistresses with whom he slakes his lust. Oh, well, yes, I *do* know the reason—he desires a legitimate male heir to pass his lands and wealth to."

"I think all husbands want that," I said, "but he should still be mindful of your wellbeing."

"Oh, he would quickly find another wife should I succumb, I am sure." Bitterness grew in her voice. "He was married once before, you know; *she* died in childbirth. Did you see that pretty red-haired maiden dancing at the banquet? His daughter Beatrix. Isn't it odd, though—he desperately wants a son, but throws only girls with his wedded wives? He has a bastard boy, Bertrand, by some frowzy harlot—that's if the child is indeed his. It hardly resembles him."

"Maybe next time you will have a boy," I said.

She shivered. "I do not want to fall pregnant right now—not while Felicia is sickly and my own body ailing. I am almost tempted to go to the village wise-woman and obtain a potion to prevent conception—just for a short while, you understand—I know such practices are sinful. But I am afraid Rotrou would find out what I'd done and punish me."

I hung my head, not sure what to say. I had done my duty by Eustace, and although he could be a hothead, he was not so inconsiderate in matters of the flesh.

"Sometimes...I dream of England," said Tilda softly. The teardrops glinted like diamonds as they clung to the long sweep of her lashes. Weak sunlight stole from the clouds and stroked the purple shadows under her eyes. "The court, as gossipy as it could sometimes be! Father. Good Queen Matilda. Little William Adelin and little Adelaide—the dear babies. And wonderful Winchester, where King Arthur once gathered with his knights at the Round Table long ago..."

Again, I had nothing to say; I was not the kind of woman who easily cooed and fussed, petting and embrace to give comfort. In my extreme youth, I had not borne Father's favour as Tilda did, for whatever reason, so I had not been thrust into glittering court life. Instead, my memories were of my mother Ansfrida changing the linen while she sang, my rough-and-tumble brothers running through the corn with an angry farmer on their heels, the village church with its familiar comforting scent of tallow mixed with frankincense and the old half-blind priest who liked to rant about hell—his name was Harold, so, behind his back, the local children called him Hellfire Hal...I missed all these things, even old Hellfire Hal's preaching, but I had consigned them to the past forever.

At that moment, there was commotion on one of the great towers soaring high above our heads. Shading my eyes against the brightness in the sky, I glanced up. Light glinted on metal helms, on the tips of arrows set to the string. "Someone is coming," I said, a surge of unease rushing through me.

"We expect no guests." Anxious, Tilda stared up at the lines of archers with bows bent. Distantly we heard the clank of the great chain lifting the portcullis—whoever had arrived must have made themselves known and were deemed fit to enter.

"I must go to see who comes," said Tilda. "It is my duty in Rotrou's absence—but oh, I wish he were here. I am not fierce enough to deal with these harsh Normans, and so many of them look upon women as little more than kine, even those of noble blood."

"I will accompany you, Tilda," I said grimly. "You will not face whoever comes alone."

"But you are with child! I could not ask you endanger both yourself and the babe!"

I patted my almost-invisible belly. "He—or she—is the Conqueror's grandchild. This child is forged from iron and fire."

We went down into the Great Hall. Servants were milling about in confusion. Taking a deep breath, Tilda sat down on her high seat upon the dais. I stood near her, almost like a guard, hoping my tallness would make me look imposing.

The steward scurried into the chamber, bowed. "My Lady, a messenger has come from Henry, King of England."

"Father!" Tilda sat bolt upright and glanced nervously over at men. Then, clearing her throat, she said in a commanding voice, "Bring in the messenger. I will meet with him. Have his companions given broth, meat and ale in the guardhouse."

The steward departed, his red robes swishing on the flagstones, and a few minutes later, Father's messenger arrived, his hair worn long in the English fashion, but tangled, his face beardless yet covered by a thick haze of stubble. Henry's Lion roared on the breast of his mud-stained tabard. He went down on one knee and proffered a rolled-up parchment to Tilda.

Carefully, she took it and broke the seal. I saw her fingers tremble. I held my breath. No one ever knew what news might come; death and illness ran rife no matter whether you were king or serf, and life was short for many—men dying through war, women through childbed, children through poxes and evil humours.

"Juliane, I cannot believe it…" Tilda's voice was low.

"What…what is it?" I feared the worst.

A small smile moved the pale lips; suddenly, she looked happier than I had seen her since I came to Perche. "Juliane, Father is coming to Normandy. He says he has had enough with Uncle Robert's plotting, and the machinations of Robert de Belleme. He will be visiting me and Rotrou—and he will also visit you in Breteuil!"

Eustace and I returned to Breteuil at once, not so much because Father was going to grace us with a royal visit, but because his missive warned us that a contingent of rebel barons, fronted by jealous Uncle Robert, the Duke of Normandy, was about to strike against those who did not support their cause.

Worst amongst these barons was Robert de Belleme, a great friend of the late William Rufus, Father's unpopular brother, from whom he had inherited the English throne. Rufus and Belleme had not always been friends but that was only expected where Belleme was concerned. He alienated everyone he met eventually—he grabbed castles, starved and mutilated prisoners, threw villeins alive into a ditch to fill it to the brim, and tore the eyes from a hostage child with his own fingernails when the boy displeased him with some childish folly. His own wife, Agnes, he despised and abused; he held her prisoner for years in Castle Belleme, until she finally managed to flee by night to the Lady Adela of Chartres, who gave her shelter.

By some stroke of evil luck, it was this Belleme who decided to pay an unexpected visit to Breteuil before my Father had reached the castle with his army. By this time, my pregnancy was quite advanced and I was resentful that this violent lord should intrude upon us. I counselled Eustace that he should not admit Belleme to our fortress, but my husband, taking council with his advisers, insisted it was best to hear Belleme out and not antagonise him.

"You don't want him at our gates with his sappers and engines, do you?" snapped Eustace when I argued that we should give no time to this man of ill-repute. "Or filling our moat with dead peasants so that he can get across to attack the walls?"

I rolled my eyes. "I just want him away from my home and my family and so should you," I said. "What do you suppose he wants?"

"What do you think most men like Belleme want? Allies!"

I sputtered with indignation. "What? You think he seeks to convince you to join his unrightful cause—against my Father, your father-in-law?"

"Yes. Robert de Belleme has no care for family ties, only for lands and mayhem. They nickname him Robert the Devil, you know. Satan himself is reputed to be his sire."

"Is he? I am sure his true sire would have something to say about that. And, for that matter, his mother."

Eustace pursed his lips. "You don't know about his mother, Mabel, do you, wife?" Next to me, my three ladies-in-waiting cackled like witches in a most uncharacteristic way. They obviously knew all about Belleme's mother and I assumed the gossip was juicy indeed.

Irritated, I waved my ladies to silence. Feigning shame, they choked back their laughter and stared sombrely at their hands. "Why would I know about this Mabel? Although she was Countess of Shrewsbury, that was long before my birth."

"Indeed. Maybe Belleme will tell you himself."

"You expect me to come into the presence of this Devil?" Annoyed, I placed my hands on my hips and glared.

"Do you wish for me to forbid you? Or keep you locked up in the highest tower of our home?" Eustace lazily stuck a grape into his mouth; he was teasing me now, despite the seriousness of the situation.

"No. It is my Father whose authority he flouts. I want to stand before him and tell him that if it is allies he wants, he will find none here at Breteuil. And if he turns out to be the Devil indeed—I will snatch the burning pitchfork from his claws and ram it into his arse."

Eustace let out a shout of mirth and grasped me around the waist. Embarrassed, the wandering pages and squires scattered in the pretext of performing useful activities—some started furiously cleaning Eustace's boots and polishing his mail, others grabbed hold of the hounds that milled about, eager for meaty scraps, and hauled them off towards the castle kennels. Cecelie, Idonea and Heloise rushed out after them in a flurry of veils.

"Ah, Juliane," Eustace said, breath hot on my cheek. "Full of fire. My heart told me you would wish to confront this baron should he come. I would expect nothing less. But if you do, I want you to swear to me…"

I opened my mouth to protest but he pressed his finger against my lips. "Swear to me, Juliane…that you will go easy on him. I don't think even the Devil's spawn can withstand you, my little firebrand."

I sniffed. "Very well, Eustace. I swear by Christ's Toenails and the Virgin's Milk, that I will give him no more trouble than a little lamb."

CHAPTER FOUR

The Devil arrived on a day black with storms. Clouds towered; ominous grumbles of thunder sounded in the distance. Standing on one of the gatehouse towers, cloaked and hooded against the rain, I spotted Belleme's banners in the distance as his entourage wound in a serpentine manner toward the castle. The emblem on his standard was a sinister black fortress set against a lurid yellow background—an unnerving insignia meant to conjure fear.

I do not fear you, I thought, as I gathered my skirts and went down to inform Eustace, but I was worried, not that Belleme would harm us, or that Eustace might fall under the spell of his reputed persuasive tongue, but fear that Father might hear of his arrival at Breteuil and believe we had betrayed him with his enemy.

Shortly after dusk, once the steward and the ostlers had stabled Belleme's horse and the steeds of his men, Robert the Devil entered the Great Hall to meet us. Eustace and I had guards on either side of the dais, stony-faced and unfriendly, wearing full mail and with swords and spears close at hand. The firepit had been filled with extra kindling, giving a warm glow to the painted walls, but there was no feast delivered to greet the newcomer. He must know from the start he was not welcome in Breteuil.

Robert de Belleme was tall and spare, dressed in black to match his evil nature. He wore a linen coif, also dyed black, and atop it a raven-hued cap with a rolled brim decorated by the images of fierce eagles, their beaks gaping and their claws outstretched. The headgear, so dark and concealing both ears and hair, gave him a strange and almost frightening appearance, for he was unnaturally pale, his cheeks as white as marble, and with all the darkness gathered around him, it made his visage float in the gloom like a severed skull, its features brought to stark prominence by its shadowy surrounds.

He halted, failing to bow or show any signs of courtesy; Eustace said nothing, but sat stiffly in his seat, his hands curled around the ends of the armrests. For a long while, or so it seemed, neither man spoke.

At length, Robert broke the uncomfortable silence. His voice was deep, harsh. "So there is no greeting, my Lord? No hospitality in your Hall? Not even the offering of a cup of peace?"

Roughly Eustace gestured for a squire to bring Belleme a goblet of wine.

"How do I know you haven't poisoned it?" asked the Baron, gazing into its depths.

"You do not," said Eustace, "but I am not in the habit of murdering my guests."

Belleme uttered a throaty laugh and drained the cup to its dregs, thrusting it rudely back at the waiting squire. "It was good." He rubbed the back of his sleeve across his mouth. "And I am still alive. My Lord Eustace, I believe you are a plain-spoken man, as I am. We do not go for this courtly nonsense that is seeping from the south."

Eustace tapped his fingers irritably on his armrest. "That may be so. Well, Lord Robert, if you are so plain-spoken, out with it then. What has brought you to Breteuil? It is not as if we were ever friends, nor was my father before me your friend."

"I will be brief and to the point. I come here because Henry, King of England, soon shall arrive in Normandy. I, like many others, including his brother Robert, Duke of Normandy, have many grievances with him." He walked a few paces forward; his boots were long, leather, finely crafted—black, of course. His cloak swung; its lining was dark red, the colour of congealed blood.

Now I could see that white, hovering face more closely. It was a cruel, odd face; angular in shape and strangely smooth for a man his age. The mouth was full but the lips had a bloodless appearance; the brows were thin and feathery while the eyes below them were a washed-out, frosty green. A snake's eyes but less warm.

"Why should I care for your grievances, my Lord?" Eustace leaned forward in his seat, frowning. "That is surely between you and the King."

Belleme's face twisted; it was fascinating and yet frightful to watch that oddly smooth skin jerk, the mouth rising in a sneer to reveal a row of sharp white teeth. "I once had many lands in England," he said. "I had a mighty fortress at a place called Bridgnorth. It stood high on a hill with the town stretching under it.

All lay below me; I would stand on the castle walls and watch over my domain and know that no other in those debatable lands could challenge the might of Belleme. However, he took it from me. Henry the Bloody First of that name. Christ's Teeth, Lord Eustace, that castle was mine, built by my own efforts!"

"Henry was angry. I cannot say I blame him. Not only was the castle unlicensed, I believe—you had led an invasion a year or two before in an attempt to put Henry's brother on the throne. I *know* these things, Lord Robert."

"You are well informed." Belleme's ice-chip gaze suddenly shifted in my direction. A cold shiver rippled down my spine. "My Lady of Breteuil is the King of England's daughter?"

I forced my gaze to become as frosty as his. "I am."

"You are like him." Belleme's smile was not pleasant.

"So I am told….but it is hardly a mysterious thing when a child takes after one parent more than the other."

"I did not mean your appearance, my Lady."

My brows lifted. "Oh, well, you've never met my mother if you think my sire is hot-tempered."

Out of the corner of my eyes, I saw my husband hide a smirk with his sleeve.

Belleme no longer smiled. He whipped away from me, lithe and deadly as a striking snake, and approached Eustace once more. "Join me," he said. "If we put Duke Robert on the throne of England—the throne that should rightfully be his as the elder brother—I swear you will come into great wealth. Greater than this…this place." He cast his gaze around the room, expression one of disdain. "Did I not hear…that you had interests in the Castle of Ivry?"

Eustace froze. That castle needled him like a thorn, Ivry. *Ivry.* He had it in his mind that it should be his, and so its grey battlements haunted his waking dreams.

"Join me and Duke Robert…and one day it will be yours." Belleme's eyes were hooded, concealing their coldness; his voice was a cat's purr, low and rumbling—but lacking a cat's affection. I felt he should have hissed instead, like an adder ready to strike.

"You Normans! So damn inquisitive!" I spat, completely unladylike but unable to confine my rage any longer.

Belleme recoiled in surprise and the 'spell' on my husband was broken. Eustace sat up in his chair and nodded toward our guest. "Your offers are not needed or wanted here, Lord Robert. My answer is no. I am loyal to the interests of King Henry. You may stay the night—or not, as you wish."

A spasm of rage passed over the Devil's features—but only for a second. The white oval of his face grew smooth, still. He bowed to Eustace, the bow exaggeratedly deep, mocking. "So be it, my Lord of Breteuil. You have spoken. Perhaps we shall meet again—maybe on the battlefield."

He gathered up his dark cloak and stormed from the Great Hall, knocking over a page boy carrying a carafe of wine. The boy landed on his bottom with a squawk, the carafe did a somersault in the air and landed on the flagstones, showering wine the hue of blood.

Immediately, I muttered, "An omen."

Eustace cast me a thunderous look; he did not brook such superstitions. "Clean it up," he ordered the sore-arsed page and his smirking fellow pageboys. "Now."

I could not sleep. The encounter with Robert de Belleme lingered in my dreams. Tossing and turning, I tangled my coverlets until they were in knots around my limbs. On their pallets on the floor, the girls were equally awake, kept so by my thrashing and sighs of discontent. They made miserable noises like mewling cats and, bleary-eyed with lack of rest, tried to press cushions over their heads to blot out the noise.

"You lot, get up," I ordered at length, ripping away the rumpled covers and swinging my legs out of my bed.

Immediately the ladies-in-waiting scrambled to their feet, their long hair flowing, their feet bare on the floor. "My Lady would dress?" asked Idonea, reaching from one of my gowns, laid out across an oaken chest.

"No. Look at the window, woman—it's still night. I, as you can tell, cannot find sleep."

Immediately they started fawning on me. "Shall I go to the herbalist?" asked Heloise. "Perhaps some valerian in a brew would help."

"I can rub your shoulders and sing, if you feel uneasy after the visit of that odious monster today," said Cecelie. She used any chance she got get to demonstrate her fine singing voice.

"No, no, I am fine. I have had enough sleep. But you—I have kept you ladies awake long enough. Move your pallets into the hall so that my movements will not disturb you."

"But Madam, we should attend you at all times!" said Heloise, concerned.

"And it's cold in the hall, and some lusty guardsman might come along and ogle us in just our kirtles," said Cecelie, crossing her arms over her chest virtuously.

"Let me know if one does and I'll have the beast flogged," I said, only half-jesting. "Do not argue, my girls. Be off with you. I don't want to see you all stumbling around tomorrow as you'd spent the night in a tavern."

My women knew they could not argue further. Silent now, they dragged their pallets and coverlets and sheepskins out into the hall. The door shut. I heard a few giggles through the stout wood—but, before long, they faded to gentle snores.

I sat in my bed for a while, leaning up against the carven headboard, wondering if I should make one final attempt to sleep. Eventually, I decided it was useless and rose and pulled on a loose over-kirtle and cloak. Leaning over as best I could with my large belly, I managed to slip into my shoes. My hair I whipped into an untidy braid, reaching almost to my waist. In all propriety, I should have worn the proper wimple of a wedded wife over it, but I did not want to rouse my ladies-in-waiting yet again, and I was not expecting to see anyone. I wanted only a short time alone to gather my thoughts about the treacherous words of Belleme. His talk of battlefield meetings—it was almost a threat. I wondered what I should tell Father when he arrived; he needed to know the worst of it, but I also knew his fiery temper. If he was extremely angry with Robert the Devil, and it was apparent he already held him in contempt, he could start a bloody war that would encompass all of Eustace's lands. He was not coming over from England for a friendly chat and a mug of ale, that I knew, but I'd rather we at Breteuil could stay away from the heart of any conflict.

Silently, I opened the bedchamber door. The ladies lay all about on their pallets, sound asleep, no doubt dreaming of the things that pleased them most—trinkets and ribbons, banquets and pavanes, lusty lords and handsome knights.

Carefully I stepped over their prone forms and sought the solace of the castle gardens. It was so early I passed no one but an old man stoking the fires, who jumped half out of his skin to see me. I wondered if Belleme had departed yet; with the normal clatter and clash of the household in the evening, I did not know—or care.

Once outside, I took deep gulps of the cold air, so chill it hurt my lungs, but refreshing after the normal castle smells of smoke, food, animals, and people. The herb-beds were damp blobs in the gloom, dewdrop-laden spiderwebs stretching across the leafy fronds like strands of jewels. Above, the keep loomed, its narrow windows rows of slitted eyes. On the farthest side of the garth, the wall and its walkway ran off into the morning mist curling around one of the watch-towers, a vaguely-outlined ghost in the greyness.

In my belly the child stirred, as if anxious. "Be still, my little one," I murmured, pressing my hand to my belly. "A few more months and you will look upon the world. Let us pray it will be a peaceful arrival."

A faint sound of boots on the path, quiet, almost furtive made me turn. My heart did an unpleasant somersault as I saw Robert de Belleme gliding towards me, visage saturnine, his ebony cloak flapping behind him in the dawn-wind. I could almost imagine that cloak becoming wings and Belleme transforming into a raven or a bat and soaring over the keep roof.

I strove to keep my composure. "You startled me, my lord. I did not expect to see you. Why are you here? This garden is off-limits to all but me, my husband and my ladies. Unless one is invited." I paused, growing stern. "And you, my lord Belleme, are not welcome."

He was near me now, those pale lips curved in an unnerving smile. "You intrigue me, Lady Juliane."

"Do I? Should I be flattered?"

"There is fire in you—you are not tame and docile, like most women."

"So I've been told. Most think that is a bad thing."

"You…you remind me of my mother, Mabel," said Belleme.

I gawped at him; the last thing I expected this sinister war-lord to say was that I reminded him of his dear old mother.

"I know little of Lady Belleme," I said, "save a few…rumours." I wasn't going to tell him whether these rumours were good or bad; in truth, I knew nothing, but I suspected.

"She was a woman of many words—most spoken with a viper's tongue. A poisoner too, once accidentally killing her husband's brother who took the wrong goblet."

I took a deep swallow of air; my head felt light. Still, my tongue ran on, as it always did. "Clumsy of her.'"

"She made good of it. She poisoned her target, Arnold de Echauffour, on the second attempt."

"Ah." I began to tremble and it wasn't merely from the cold. How I wished one of my ladies would show her usual nosiness and come to my rescue. Or better yet, Eustace, with a sore head and a sharpened sword…

"She will harm no one anymore," said Belleme with a strange cheerfulness, hooking his thumbs into his leather belt.

"She has repented of her crimes?"

"No. She is dead." His shoulders shook with faint mirth; I was appalled—he laughed at the demise of his own mother, truly a sin, wicked though she might have been in life. "Her enemies came upon her in the bath. They struck off her head with a blade."

My eyes grew wide, my breathing ragged. "Why do you tell me these horrors, sir? And I do not think your comparison of me to Mabel de Belleme was complimentary."

"You are too bright to do nought but breed for that sad little man, Eustace de Pacy. You are also too bright, surely, to trust your father as you clearly do. Join with me, Juliane—with my strength and your spirit…"

"What of your wife?" I said, my tone acid.

"She ran away. I am sure an annulment can be arranged with a bit of bribery to the Holy Father. Or, who knows, an accident might happen. One cannot predict accidents…"

"You are foul. You are indeed the Devil's son," I hissed in revulsion. "I will not listen to your words."

"Do you fear I'll put you under a spell?" he laughed. It was not a warm laugh but a mocking one.

"I have had enough!" Drawing on all my courage, I stared straight into those cold, pitiless green eyes. They were like serpents' eyes, unblinking. "Go, leave my home…before I call the castle guard. Remember, you are separated from your men. You are as much in danger from me as I am from you, Robert de Belleme,"

He stood silently for a moment, still piercing me with his frosty gaze. He licked his wind-dried lips; I was reminded of the way a snake's tongue flickers.

"You are a fool, Juliane FitzRoy," he said. "You should have joined me and your uncle the Duke, who should have been rightful King of England. Do you truly believe your father loves you? You are just meat to him, to be thrown to the wolves of Normandy who might otherwise bite him. Do you suppose if you were ugly, your teeth rotted and your skin pocked, that he would ever have acknowledged you or married you to Eustace de Breteuil? You'd have starved in some shite-filled ditch in England! One day…one day…" His black-gloved hand coiled into a fist; for a moment, I feared he might strike me. But he held back, although he leaned forward until his hot breath scored my cheek. "One day, woman, you will see what your sire truly is. Do you think me a sorcerer? Well, then, that is something I do foretell."

With that, he gathered his cloak around him and stormed from the garden. I waited to make sure he was definitely gone and not lying in wait, and then fled for my apartments. Inside, Heloise, Cecelie and Idonea were just rising, yawning and stretching on their pallets. I flew past them, making torches and candleflames shiver and dip. My heart was pounding; I was not a woman given to crying but I felt hot tears sting my eyelids. My hands were quaking like those of a crone.

"My Lady, what is it?" Heloise shrieked, rushing to my side and steadying me. "What has happened?"

I gulped back sobs, rubbing at my eyes, struggling to regain my composure. "It is nothing, Heloise—just womanish folly due to my expectant state."

Gundrada came hobbling in, having heard the commotion. Tutting, she forced me towards the bed. "You lie down, my dearest Lady," she ordered, casting my ladies-in-waiting a look that dared them to come any closer. Although she was retired from my service, she still bore a deep attachment to me, and woe betide any of my maids who got in her way.

"I will go get a posset for you," she soothed. "Lie still now."

I did as she bade and listened as I heard the sound of many hooves drumming in the bailey and the squeal of the portcullis being raised. Robert de Belleme and his company were gone, thanks be to God.

CHAPTER FIVE

King Henry's expected visit came the next month. He had visited Tilda and Rotrou and other barons before swinging round to Breteuil. He came riding into the castle courtyard with his company of chosen knights, while the rest of his men camped on the slopes outside the fortress, their pavilions garlanded with banners, the endless streams of baggage trains rowdy with whores and other camp followers.

He swaggered into the Great Hall still clad in mail, his face heavily bearded and sweat-stained. "Juliane, my daughter!" he roared, grasping me and swinging me about as if we had been close all our lives, which was neither true nor ever expected by a bastard-child. "You look fairer to the eye than ever! And…" he eyed my expanding belly, "you are soon to give me another grandson!"

"I am hoping it will be a granddaughter," I said with a little smile.

"Ah, yes, yes, you women always want girls to fritter away your time with."

I said nothing; I must not dishonour my father by arguing—especially as all the good things of my life had come from his largesse. "How is her Grace the Queen?"

"Holy as ever. Washing the feet of the poor and sick, founding leper hospitals and abbeys. Praying for my success in Normandy, of course. She is a good woman."

"Yes. And my half-brother the Prince? And Princess Adelaide?"

"Well. Thriving. Adelaide is the toughest little girl I have ever met—and I've met many." He roared in mirth, slapping his thighs." I swear she would rather wield a sword than a sewing needle. A little like you, as I recall, Juliane…or has Eustace beaten such foolishness out of you?" He released another bellow of laughter.

"He has done no such thing, my Lord King," I said indignantly.

"He seems to have grown into a stalwart enough man." Father glanced over at Eustace, who was entertaining some of the King's friends, Robert FitzHamon and Gilbert FitzRichard. "I had my doubts, I will tell you—but perhaps I am proved wrong."

"You had doubts, but sent me to him anyway?"

"That's what my pretty daughters are for. Making blood-ties that bind. And you are doing your duty by the look of things." Suddenly he grasped me and kissed my brow. "You are a good girl, Juliane. You and Tilda will make sure your husbands hold fast for me." He stepped back, the embrace broken. "Now…I will go and be bathed and dressed in the manner of a King. Pah, I smell like a dead horse, and no surprises there, for two died beneath me as I rode hence to see my sweet Juliane."

The rest of Father's visit was spent with Eustace and the local nobility. I was not invited to any meetings, which irked me deep in my heart, but my exclusion, as a female, was not unexpected. I wanted to tell the King about Belleme's threats but I dared not with my husband in the room. He would go mad and start his own campaign against Robert the Devil, and I knew, deep within my heart, that Eustace would prove no match for the former Earl of Shrewsbury.

So I had to content myself with paying off servants in the hall to repeat snatches of talk overheard amongst the lords. It seemed my Father's position was strong. He had confronted Uncle Robert at Domfront, many great barons at his back, and told his brother he was aware he had raised trouble against him. He had promised to bring fire and sword to Normandy if Robert continued with his scheming. Robert had backed down and promised he would hold to the Treaty of Alton.

I sighed in relief. If my Uncle's words were genuine, then Robert de Belleme's power would be reduced; he would have to retreat to Castle Belleme to sulk—and plot—on his own.

Father summoned me the next day. He was in a jolly and generous mood and gave a silver cup full of coins to my little son, William, whom he dandled on his knee. "A fine lad," he said, "named after my doughty father and looking much like him too. But you should have named him Henry."

"Eustace's father was William, and he admired the Conqueror as all men should. Maybe next time, Sire. With luck, I will have many healthy children."

"Aye, with luck and the generosity of God Almighty." He called for a servant and the man brought forth a small chest of cedarwood. Opening it, the King took out a fine girdle of golden threads. "For you, my daughter, a gift. Keep young Eustace sweet—and loyal. Although Robert is quiet enough now, I am not fool enough to think his peace will last. But for now, I must hasten back to England."

He departed, horns blaring in his wake, and galloped down the high hill and along the lakeshore. I watched him, waving from the tallest turret of Castle Breteuil. As I did, my unborn child leapt strongly, almost uncomfortably, in my womb. I staggered a little, feeling light-headed and unbalanced.

"My Lady, please, come down from the heights." Cecelie tugged insistently on my sleeve, her pert face white with worry.

I began to descend the tower stairs; rain had leaked into the tower and funnelled down the stone spiral leading to the lower level. I tried to take extra care, stepping gingerly into the gloom, but perhaps my over-caution made my tentative steps less sure, rather than more.

Beneath my thin slippers, the wet stonework felt as smooth as glass. I gasped, stumbled forward, clutching futilely at slippery stone walls. Cecelie screamed and tried to grab hold of me but I fell like a stone, rolling down the spiral stairs in a flurry of skirts and gown. I flung my arms across my middle, attempting to protect the child. Above, I could see the sky through the door onto the turret growing further and further away, a patch of light laced with clouds.

And then my head struck hard upon a jut of brutal stone, and the light faded into utter darkness.

The baby was born early in a welter of blood and pain through which I drifted in and out of consciousness, sometimes waking with screams on my lips, the room spinning; at other times sinking into a merciful, poppy-laced darkness. A priest was called at one point; I heard his gravelly voice as he muttered the last rites. I could not weep or feel to protest that I would live, *wanted* to live; I clutched Gundrada's gnarled old claw and let darkness wrap me round again.

But I did not die. I was ill for a very long time, both from loss of blood and from the blow to my skull. I remember little of that time, for I was so weak. I could barely even ask as to the fate of my child. Sometimes I dreamed of a baby clad in white robes, shining like an angel...but it was borne away by a black bat that had the scowling visage of Robert de Belleme. I wondered if the rumours about his deviltry were true and he had cursed me...

And then I woke, feeling weak but in my right mind. And I knew I would not die. God had spared my life. It was dusk outside and pale blue light filled the chamber. Next to my bed, Gundrada slumped on a stool, snoring, a thin trickle of drool running from her mouth onto her white apron.

"Gundrada," I croaked. "Water...bring me water. Oh God, I am hungry too."

The old woman made a snorting noise and her heavy eyelids sprang open. "Jesu be praised! You are back in the world of the living, my poor Lady Juliane."

I struggled to sit; my limbs felt heavy as lead. "The babe...what of my babe? It...it was too soon."

Gundrada stared at the flagstones and shook her head.

A sob tore at my throat. "Was he baptised? Oh, please tell me that he was!" I dreaded to think of the poor little soul damned for all time.

"The priest who came to give you extreme unction baptised the babe at the same time. But any of the midwives were ready to do it—the Church allows such a mercy."

Exhausted, grief-filled, I fell back against the pillow. "The child, it was..."

"A boy, another boy. Lord Eustace has seen that he was buried in the local church beneath a decorated slab. The villagers place wildflowers on it."

Tears leaked down my face; I had never felt so weak, so wretched.

Gundrada dabbed at the tears with a grimy kerchief—her own, I deemed. I was too feeble to push the rag away. "It was God's will, my dear one. Fear not, you will surely bear another babe in good time."

"Where is my husband?" I asked.

"I shall get him for you, my Lady." Gundrada tucked her kerchief into her apron and hobbled away.

A short while later, Eustace entered the bedchamber alone. He looked windswept as if he'd been out riding, and his face bore an uncomfortable expression. Like most men, he did not fare well in women's matters or in situations where tears might fall.

"Juliane...wife." His hand clutched mine. "I am so glad you have returned to yourself."

"I will recover from this terrible ordeal. I will bear you more children, Eustace!"

"Do not even speak of children right now." His expression was horrified. "You are too frail."

"But what if...if something should happen to our little Will..."

"Nothing will happen to him," he said fiercely, fists clenching. "I beg you do not speak so, lest you bring ill-luck on the household."

I already wondered if I had done so by verbally sparring with Robert de Belleme in the garden. I should not have let him near me, kept his foul, fetid breath from blowing, like a miasma of poison, onto my face. I should have immediately screamed, raised the alarm, and had him and his minions driven from Castle Breteuil on the points of spears. But I would not tell Eustace of ill-starred meeting. No one must ever know.

"The...the baby...Gundrada tells me he was duly baptised before he died. What was he named?"

"Ralph."

"Ralph." A name that was not common in my family but, I surmised, his. I was secretly glad he had not called the dead infant Henry, although there would have been no problem with naming another son Henry later on. But it would have felt wrong somehow—unlucky.

"Ralph was brother to my father."

I shook my head; I'd never heard of the man.

"He died young too."

I lay back in silence. "Leave me. I am weary."

He had no words of comfort; all these Normans were hard men in that way. Not that I wanted comfort. Now I just wanted to grow strong again. As the Lady of Breteuil and a King's daughter, I must not show weakness. I must stand as strong as the castle walls.

By midsummer the worst of my illness had passed. The Pope had granted a dispensation so I could eat meat on fast days, and its rich goodness helped my health return. After a period of seclusion, cloistered away with my three ladies and Gundrada, where I did nought but embroider and read my Psalter and walk in my private garden, I returned to the hall to eat at Eustace's side and joined my husband in hunting and hawking forays—and in the bedchamber.

Soon I was my usual self, nosy and opinionated about the state of affairs in Normandy. Despite the agreements of last year, trouble had bubbled up yet again. Father's friend, Robert Fitzhamon, had fared across the Channel with a small company, seeking to confront Uncle Robert over new suspicions of treachery. Showing his perfidious nature, the Duke took Fitzhamon prisoner and chained him up in a grim fortress in Bayeux.

Father was enraged but jubilant too. It was the perfect excuse to invade Normandy.

"Do you think the King will cross the Narrow Sea?" I asked Eustace.

"Yes, without doubt" replied Eustace. "FitzHamon is a firm favourite; you saw the honour the King did him when the royal party was in Breteuil. He will come—and I will go to assist him, as is my sworn duty."

"Eustace, my dear husband, I am so proud of your loyalty." I stretched up to set a feather-light kiss upon his lips. And I *was* proud, but I felt fearful too. Eustace had never known war before. "I wish I could don mail and ride along beside you with a sword in my hand."

"And make me a laughing-stock?" he cried, incredulous.

"I was but jesting. You never seem to understand my jests, Eustace," I frowned, folding my arms in mock annoyance.

He drew me closer to him, his arms like iron bands around my waist. "There is only one battle you might win, my sweet lady." We were in the privacy of our solar. "And that is in the bedchamber, and even then…"

"Let us put it to the test," I whispered against the curve of his ear, letting my hand trail down his chest and then lower across his belly. I was a young woman, and fertile—I desperately wanted another baby to replace the one I had lost. A huge household of healthy children was my aim; I had no wish to be like my poor sister Tilda, still with only two girls, one sickly, and a husband who had lost interest as he cavorted with his mistresses and spawned umpteen bastards.

Eustace made a grunting noise and taking my hand, dragged me behind the screen for some semblance of privacy. We coupled like beasts, standing upright despite the prohibitions of the Church, who claimed it was a sinful position. My back rubbed against the wall; my heels banged the floor. It was passionate, ungentle…and over quickly, leaving us both weak and breathless.

"My Lady," he said when he was done, breath railing through his lungs, "I leave you with that to remember me when I am away at your sire's war!"

He departed for Bayeux the next day, riding at the head of his gathered troops. I did not wave farewell from the topmost tower as I once would have done; I would not climb up to the spot where I had my accident ever again.

I did not know it then but he had left me with more than memories of stolen passion. He had left me with my desire—another child.

It was difficult keeping both calm and busy in Eustace's absence. He was not a man who knew his letters well, so he could not write. I stayed in the castle, sick to my belly due to my quickening, irritated by the constant twitter of my three ladies, and wishing I could have travelled to Bayeux with my husband, even if I was part of the baggage and had to be dropped off at a safe distance from the battlefield. But no, that was a foolish thought. I must protect this new babe as I had not protected poor, lost Ralph, my failing and my sorrow. Whenever I closed my eyes, I saw the tower's spiral stairs and the sky at the top vanishing into the distance as I fell—and, in my worst moments, I even imagined Robert de Belleme's marble-pale visage twisted with malignant mirth as he looked down at me, willing me to fall, to enter eternity...

Finally, a messenger arrived, bearing joyous news to the household. Major battles had taken place, Robert FitzHamon was free, and Eustace, hale and unscathed, was returning home to Breteuil.

It was now nearly Christmas. Skies were grey and the water of the lake that stretched below the castle walls iced over. On some nights a thin drizzle of snow fell, frosting the red slates that roofed the castle turrets. Fires burned constantly on the hearths and the air smelled of woodsmoke and ash mingled with greenery—the servants had begun to decorate the Great Hall for the upcoming Yule-tide festivities. Boughs of evergreen cast off a rich scent to counter the acrid smoke; holly berries, red as beads of blood, brightened the fuggy gloom. The household sang as they worked, looking forward to the end of Advent when they could break their long fast, worship the Christ Child, and make merry through till Twelfth Night.

I worked too, as much as my pregnancy allowed it—visiting the kitchens and the pantry and making sure we had the required food for the Christmas feast. My head swam with thoughts of geese and boar, pike and salmon, frumenty and tarts. I arranged for mummers to arrive, called in the best minstrels and even hired a Fool named Raoul, who had a wicked wit.

When Eustace came riding past the lake and up through the town gates with the villagers crowded around, cheering him on, my heart leapt in admiration, love and excitement, but when he finally entered my solar and dismissed my ladies-in-waiting with a curt nod, my heart began to sink.

He looked a different man. Older, more careworn, his were cheeks sunken and his eyes hollowed. His hair had not been washed for weeks and someone had cut it with a knife so that it stood up in greasy clumps.

I rose from my seat to greet him. "Eustace, husband. what is wrong? Is it not a victory?"

"What have you heard, Juliane?" He flung off his cloak, leaking water, before the firepit and threw himself on a bench.

"I heard there were battles; Bayeux was burnt. Caen surrendered. Father convinced Uncle Robert to submit to his will again and now he has returned to England."

A terrible expression crossed Eustace's visage. I had never seen such a look on his face before. He could wax proud and haughty, he could love blood like most of his fellow Normans, but I had never seen such hot rage in his eyes.

"You are frightening me!" I cried, my voice embarrassingly shrill. I grasped the fine blue beads of the rosary which was attached to my girdle of silver wires; the feel of the smooth glass was strangely comforting, calming.

"Let me tell you about your Father's little foray to rescue his friend, FitzHamon, shall I?" Without waiting for an answer, Eustace began to rage on: "Bayeux was firmly in Duke Robert's camp and held out long behind its stalwart gates. The King grew enraged, as he felt he was losing control of Caen while he waited outside Bayeux with no talk of surrender from the besieged. So, he summoned one of his supporters, Count Helias, who marched from Le Mans with a mighty host. Mercenaries also joined the army and when the ranks had swelled to a size Henry thought adequate, we attacked Bayeux. The gates fell, the great battering rams brought by Helias taking them down…"

"You were there when they fell?"

"Of course I was! The King rode through the streets of Bayeux, and as he proceeded, he shouted for the town to be fired, burnt to the ground. You should have seen it, Juliane—a vision of Hell. Chapels and churches engulfed in flame, their roofs collapsing in ruins, their bells falling from their belfries with booms like thunder. Women and children screaming, pursued like cattle by the mercenaries while their homes were destroyed and the town's food-stores toppled into the streets. The mercenaries grabbed at the food like ravening beasts, just as they grabbed at the women, taking whatever they could carry. The King had promised it to them, you see."

Eustace's lips curved in a sneer. I stayed silent; I did not like the disparaging tone of his voice when he spoke of Father. Bad blood had come between them.

My husband stared up at the ceiling; his hands were clenching and unclenching. I noticed his knuckles were cut, his hands rimed with bruises; he had seen action. "There was one church, Juliane, an episcopal church that was extremely wealthy. The men of Le Mans surrounded it, dragged the clergy outside then torched the roof. The church was full of relics and icons of gold and silver, and some priests ran back into the smoke and flame to haul the treasures out. They laid them on the cobblestones, weeping like babes, their faces and hair singed by the fire, and begged that the goods remain in their hands..."

"And the King refused and gave them to the mercenaries."

"And the men of Le Mans," said Eustace bitterly.

I had to admit surprise. I had not thought Eustace so pious that he should care overmuch of the fate of the clergy. Gently I put my hand on his shoulder. "It grieves me you had to see men of God rudely treated, but such is the way of war..."

His face twisted again and he pulled away from my touch with frightening abruptness. "Rudely treated? Those self-righteous shave-heads commanded the townsfolk to hold the gate; they should have swung for their crime! What pains me is that the King gave all the choicest rewards to Count Helias and his sell-swords. I got nothing..."

I recoiled, disappointed in his outburst. I was seeing an unpleasant side to him I had occasionally noticed before—a tendency to fret and stew when something he thought was rightfully his lay beyond his grasp. An inclination to envy.

"You do not need stolen goods, Eustace," I said, unable to keep the coldness from my voice. "We are not poor. Let the hire-swords have it. It belonged to the church; stealing it will bring nothing good."

"No, I don't need pilfered plate and gemstones, I suppose," Eustace's voice was a nasty whip-crack. "The King literally told me as much. Told me I already had my reward—my own father's castles at Pacy and Breteuil—such a grand prize for a lowly bastard!—and a King's byblow to wife."

I began to tremble at his venomous words, which tore at my very soul. In no wise would I have expected his homecoming to bring such bitterness and vitriol. There I was, imagining victory celebrations, a happy Eustace fresh from his first military endeavours, high in the favour of his father-in-law and the lords of the land! Instead *this*...

My husband still had not finished his rant about the campaign. "And to think—I will doubtless have to go through this humiliation again next year!"

"Next year?" I shook my head, not understanding. "Is there not peace? Has not Duke Robert bent his knee to my father?"

"Robert Curthose is a faithless whoreson!" Eustace roared, making me step backwards with his unexpected vehemence. Spittle from his lips wet my cheek. "He has sworn oaths before and cast them aside within days. He will not bow to Henry of England, his younger brother. He wants the English crown as well as the Dukedom of Normandy, all men know that. Your father should never have taken his word…"

"What else could he have done?" I said helplessly.

Eustace's teeth gritted. "Imprisoned him. Or better, yet, killed him!"

"Eustace!"

"Do not act so shocked, wife. All men know Henry most likely had a hand in the death of William Rufus in the New Forest. If he killed one brother, why not the other too? All his problems would be over."

"That…that is a wicked, foolish thing to say! I pray you have not said such things to any others," I gasped. "Oh yes, I know of the rumours about Father's involvement with Rufus's demise—but all are unproven and I would never dare speak of them to man or woman. To do so, would be dangerous, even for me, Henry's daughter. Far more dangerous still for a bastard-born Count's son who holds his lands through the King's good graces!"

His hand shot out, a dark blur moving like lightning. He struck my left cheek, sending me reeling back a few steps. "How dare you, madam?"

My eyes blazed as my face reddened both from the force of his slap and from the humiliation of his blow. "How dare *you* raise hand to a woman with child? Your child!"

He blustered and babbled then, making no sense, anger mingled with regret, embarrassment and guilt. I glanced away, unable to meet those strained, bloodshot eyes. Eyes that barely seemed familiar in that moment.

"I will retire to my chambers, if it please you," I said frostily.

"Yes, yes," he muttered, staring at the flagstones, as he paced like a trapped beast. "I will have my dinner alone. I need a good stew or venison pie in my belly to chase away the winter's cold and put me in a better temper."

Nervous, I swallowed, stepping uncomfortably from one foot to the other, afraid of arousing his wrath again. "I must remind you, Eustace, it is Advent, and also Tuesday, an Ember day. All you can eat on an Ember day is fish, vegetables, and eggs…"

"Jesu!" he shouted, and in frustration, he grabbed a burning log from the fire and dashed it on the floor. Sparks sailed out as the wood disintegrated and landed amidst the dry rushes that coated the ground.

"Eustace, have you gone mad? You'll burn the castle down!" I shrieked, falling to my knees and beating at sparks with my hands. "Your sire's home. *Our* home, with our little son William in it!"

Eustace had grabbed his sopping cloak and started to smother what remained of the embers, his motions jerky and wrathful. He refused to glance in my direction.

Cheek still stinging from his unexpected blow, I fled the chamber without glancing back. Christmas at Breteuil was, at least for me, cancelled.

Over the following months Eustace and I were reconciled, but I never felt quite at ease with my husband again. His brief taste of war seemed to have awakened an unpleasant longing in him, greater than in the past—for what other men owned. I had seen it when we first met when he spoke of possessing Ivry and was not content with his own generous lot. A ruthlessness developed within him as well; the old ruffians of his youth appeared at the castle once again, and he spent long hours talking about killing his enemies and appropriating their lands and castles.

I was concerned with less violent pursuits, and in the spring gave birth to a healthy baby girl. Eustace sent gifts to the birthing chamber but was more interested in his plotting and planning than in a girl-child; it was I who chose a name that I deemed rare and beautiful—Lora—a feminine version of the name of blessed Saint Lawrence, who died horribly upon a gridiron.

It turned out that Eustace was correct about one thing, however; my Uncle Robert was back to his usual ham-fisted treachery, and it was apparent that it was only a matter of time before the King moved his armies across the Channel yet again. I was pleased to find out, however, that his hasty departure after taking Caen was not because, as Eustace suggested, that he had foolishly taken Robert's word as truth, but because he was in a wrangle with Archbishop Anselm, who had been in exile for many years. Fearing excommunication, he had to agree to give Anselm back the revenue of Canterbury, and also agree that in the future Bishops could not marry, which would probably cause a stir amongst those already with wives and children, but there was no helping it—the law had changed.

Despite his original rage at the prospect of more military action, for which I had suffered the back of his hand, Eustace began to look forward to going to war. My husband had changed twice since we were wed, first from a gauche boy to a straightforward young lord, and now to a man hungering for martial pursuits and other men's lands. I was not pleased by the nature of this change, but as a woman, I could say nothing; it was not my place. I was confined to the nursery with William and Lora and tried to take my pleasure from their childish antics and from my gardens and rides along the lakeside with Cecelie and Idonea—Heloise had wed a young knight and had gone to another town to start a new life. The solar was quieter without the threesome chattering, and I cannot pretend, although I liked all the girls, that I did not savour my newfound peace, with minstrels playing sweet airs in the background instead of constant shrieks and chatter.

Eustace rode out with his levies, as before, but since Bayeux, his forces had swollen threefold and he proceeded with new-found confidence, even eagerness. I doubt it was so much to help my Father against Duke Robert, as to fully ingratiate himself once and for all and get the rewards he thought were his just desserts.

He was heading to a place called Tinchebrai.

News came from the battlefield early in October. I had gone hawking by the lake with Cecelie and Idonea. We galloped on our palfreys along the shore; the water was still, mirroring a rich blue sky, while gold and red leaves danced across the surface, swirling like little boats as the wind took them. My Merlin hawk, Desiree, was abroad in the sky, swooping and wheeling and screeching. I sat astride my white mare, watching the hawk's flight, my damson hood with its fox-fur trim thrown back to reveal my head, decently covered but only with thin veiling held in place by a jewelled band, the same one Queen Matilda had given me for my wedding day.

"Oh, look, Desiree is after something!" squealed Idonea, squinting into the sky as she shaded her eyes with a gloved hand.

The rest of our party, squires, pages, grooms, falconers began to murmur and gaze skyward.

Desiree let out a fearsome cry and descended through the clear air like an arrow shot from the string. A faint blurry shape swooped before her, wings beating furiously. A songbird, seeking its escape, seeking to live another day.

It would not. My falconer was excellent and Desiree trained well.

Releasing another shrill screech, the Merlin pursued the fleeing songbird with intent, grasping it in her strong, sharp talons. There was a commotion in the heavens and a cloud of feathers spiralled earthwards, making Cecelie and Idonea laugh as they brushed their upturned faces. They tried to catch the fluffy pieces, soft grey.

Desiree had her prey on the ground now, pecked and bloodied. I beckoned to the Falconer and he lifted up the hawk, her bells jingling merrily as he slipped her hooded jesses upon her, bringing her under full control.

"The prey—let me see what she has brought me," I ordered. "You, squire…."

One of the squires, Thierry, a tall pimply-faced boy with a yellow bowl of hair, picked up the dead bird and gingerly carried it over.

"It is very small, my Lady," said Idonea, peering over my shoulder as I examined the dead bird. "It would not make two mouthfuls."

"Ah, but what pleasant mouthful," I said, with a smile, "Desiree has brought us an Ortolan, a delightful meal for one. Roman emperors used to blind these birds with pins so that, locked forever in darkness, they would gorge on seeds and grow fat. To prepare them, the cook must roast the Ortolan briefly, feathers still on, then pluck what is left before serving."

"Wrap up the Ortolan, Thierry." I turned to the squire. "Bear it back to the castle kitchens. Tell Cook I shall have it at table tonight."

The boy went to take Desiree's prey from my hand but just as his fingers clasped it, he slipped on the sodden leaves that clung in a golden haze to the muddy paths around the lake. The dead Ortolan flew up into the air as Idonea and Cecelie gasped in dismay. Instinctively, I reached down from my horse, snatching the bird before its tiny corpse hit the ground. Blood smeared my hand, dripped onto the silvered billows of my skirts.

"Your expensive glove!" wailed Cecelie. "It is ruined!"

Annoyed, I opened my mouth to chide her for her foolish outburst, but closed it again with a snap. As I turned my head, I had seen something unexpected—something that would need my attention.

The castle steward was riding along the lakeside toward our party. Beside him rode a stranger in dusty garb who clearly had been on the road for many days. A messenger.

I halted, clutching the Ortolan, as the last of its life's blood drained away, staining my garments with scarlet.

I sat on the dais in the Great Hall, the messenger before me in new garments that I had ordered the Chamberlain, Robert de Maine, to supply. After I had ascertained that my husband was alive and unharmed, I had sent de Maine to find the man food and have him washed and dressed—he had smelt of horse, rank sweat and old urine. I suspected he had scarcely stopped along the road in his haste to bring news from the battlefield.

"So, man, what is your name?" I said kindly. I snapped my fingers for a page to bring him a mug of ale. He drank it thirstily; his lips were cracked and dry.

"Hugues, my Lady Juliane," he said. "Hugues de Courtenay."

"Hugues, speak then. I take it that this time it is an outright victory for the King."

"It is, Countess. All is changed in Normandy. At Tinchebrai, a great battle was fought. Duke Robert is duke no more and is in the custody of his Grace, King Henry of England!"

"Uncle Robert—captured at last!" I wondered what Father would do to him; fraternal love was not very great in our family. A knife as quick as a kiss.

Hugues nodded. "King Henry and his allies laid siege to the Castle of Tinchebrai, standing high upon a hill and held by Robert's supporter, William of Mortain. Duke Robert arrived with his army but he could not lift the siege. He decided to challenge his brother to do battle upon the plain below the castle. Knowing his army was greater, Henry readily agreed. Soon it was clear that his Grace had won the day. He had many supporters: Tosney, Montfort, Beaumont, Warrenne, Alan Duke of Brittany and others—including the good Lord of Bretieul, Eustace. Robert had but two adherents of any note—Mortain and Robert de Belleme."

I shivered at the sound of the Devil's name and clapped my hands to my ears. "Do not speak of that spawn of evil—Satan's own." My heart suddenly filled with hope and I grabbed his sleeve. "Belleme...does he yet live?"

"I am afraid so, Lady. He was in the rear-guard and fled when the battle turned against Duke Robert. He was ever most mindful of his own skin."

I frowned. "This does not surprise me. I would have paid you extra coin if you had brought me the good news that Belleme's head was on a spike before the gates of this Tinchebrai!"

"I wish I could have done so, Lady," the messenger said with a wry grin. "I have other good news that may cheer my Lady, however. Not only is the Duke taken, but Mortain. The King swears neither of them shall ever walk free again."

Shivers rippled down my spine; I pretended it was merely caused by a draft from the doorway. *Never go free again.* Life imprisonment, or...

"It was a great Victory, Countess Juliane—I have never seen such a battle before. The King used a new tactic…"

"And what was that?"

"He dismounted."

"*What*?" I was surprised. Norman cavalry was feared throughout France, and it had helped win the day for my grandsire, William the Bastard, when he took England for his own.

"Yes, and as he did so, his knights followed suit. The infantry, led by their commander, William of Evreux, charged the lines of Duke Robert, taking them by surprise. Great in number, they tore through Curthose's cavalry and brought many of their horses down, taking the knights prisoner. The Duke's forces were broken, then swept away like driftwood on a strong tide."

"Was my husband in this charge?" I asked eagerly. Eustace was always seeking favour; it might sweeten his mood if Father rewarded him for his prowess in some way. Some plunder, a minor castle…

"I did not see him, my Lady," said the messenger without meeting my eyes. "All I know is that he is hale and will return when he may."

Eustace returned a month or two after Tinchebrai had been fought. Where he had been in the meantime, he never said and I had no wish to ask. His temper was scarcely sweeter than after his first battle supporting Father. "The King should have killed Robert outright—what if he escapes?" he muttered. "He will seek out Belleme and raise another force."

"He will not escape," I said, shaking my head. We were in our bedchamber and I was bathed and rouged and scented, seeking to please my lord after his long absence. My woman's ruse did not seem to be working. Eustace wanted only to grizzle about Father. At least he did not seem inclined to slap me again—a small mercy.

"You are so certain?" His brows were raised; with his dagger-tip, he spiked a piece of pork on the trencher lying before him and thrust it aggressively into his mouth. It bulged in the side of his unshaven cheek; I was suddenly reminded of a squirrel gathering nuts for its winter store and had to bite back a peal of laughter. He certainly *would* strike me if he knew what I'd been thinking!

I pressed a kerchief to my mouth, hiding my mirth with a false cough. "Yes, I am certain, husband. I have heard it rumoured Robert will go to Devizes. It is a very strong castle and in the middle of nowhere; should he escape, the locals are so wild—heathens who worship stones, I've heard—that they would surely devour him if they caught him!"

At this, Eustace's eyes crinkled; at last, he allowed himself a small laugh. "What a fate that would be. A royal Norman eaten by savage Englishmen."

"But..." his visage darkened again; he stabbed his dagger into the tough bread of the trencher, "it is not just Robert escaping that I fear. The man has a son."

"Yes, William Clito." My cousin. "I wouldn't worry about him; he is but a child of four."

"Children grow."

"He was taken in Falaise after the battle, was he not? Transferred to the household of his half-sister Eva, who had married Helias of Saint Saens, the Count of Arque."

"Another stupid move by your Father." That awful sneer that Eustace sometimes wore appeared, making my heart grow heavy. "Helias was Robert's supporter."

"It is easier and wiser, I deem, to make former enemies your friends," I said carefully.

Eustace flung back his head, full of mocking mirth. "Spoken like a true woman—without any knowledge of reality. An enemy is an enemy, Juliane. Circumstances might lead to dealing with such as Helias, but to trust him with the son of your sworn enemy, one who would unthrone you if he could? Foolish, very foolish!"

"Let us not argue," I mumbled. I buried myself amidst the cushions on which I sat, hugging them for comfort.

"No, let us not." He seemed to calm. "I do not want to hear any more female blatherings about...men's business. Tell me about the things our son got up to in my absence, and little Lora. Give me gossip that has gone about the castle while I was at war."

"I do not like gossip," I said, "and…" I was growing a little angry, "if you wanted a wife who has no brain in her head, who sits drinking milk and honey and scarcely knows whether it is day or night…you should have forgotten about marrying a King's daughter and found one of your wide-hipped Norman broodmares with her eyes swivelled toward the ground like those of a slave!"

Open-mouthed, Eustace stared at me. The dagger in his hand fell to the table with a clunk. I clutched my embroidered cushion even closer, wondering if I had gone too far but not the least apologetic for my outburst.

Luckily, Eustace did not react with wrath; instead, he cast me a pained look. "Christ, no, I do not want an insufferable, empty-headed goose for a wife. But neither do I want a raging Amazon. Do you understand, Juliane?"

I worried my lower lip with my teeth. It seemed I did not understand *anything* about my husband anymore. Changed, and ever-changing; I could hardly keep up.

"Here…maybe this will please you." Reaching to his belt, he drew from a pouch a jewelled wrist-band. It was old and worn, the gems studded across it rubbed smooth by many fingers. Of Byzantine design, it was very beautiful. Taking my hand with surprising gentleness, he slipped it on to my wrist. "Do you like it, Juliane?"

I stared at the bracelet; a big cabochon as blue as my eyes, an emerald-green stone, a chunk of amber rich as melted honey, with a small winged bug trapped at its heart. "It is wonderful. Where did you obtain such a magnificent piece? It looks like it should be someone's prized heirloom."

Folding his arms over his chest, his face became shuttered. "You ask too many unnecessary questions. Let us just say, it was payment for my troubles…"

Looting then. So you got your wish…I turned the piece upon my wrist, my hair falling forward like a black shroud to hide my less than enthusiastic expression.

"Don't look that way, Juliane …it was mine by right. Your own father sanctioned the actions of his armies after the battle. The supporters of Duke Robert had to be punished. Here—give it back then if you are too squeamish to wear it, you ungrateful…" His face was flaming.

"No, no, I will keep it. I shall wear it to mark your battles and your transition into the highest echelons of manhood." I prayed he did not hear the sarcasm creeping into my voice; I doubted he would, for I noticed such comments ofttimes whirred over his head without comprehension.

His rage subsided; he was weary, grey streaks looped below his eyes. "I have had enough of this day. To bed…" He made as if to rise and leave.

I caught his sleeve, drawing him back; the pilfered bracelet glowed with deep rich colours against my skin and I felt a little guilty. Perhaps I had been somewhat churlish regarding his gift. I must do my best to hold on to our marriage, which so long ago had such a promising start. I needed to—for I feared what Eustace might get himself into without my calming influence.

"Do not leave me, husband," I said in a whisper, reaching up to stroke his stubbly cheek. "I have missed you these long months. Missed you more than you know."

"Truly?" His raised his brows as if he thought I was mocking him. This time, I was not. Perhaps, instead, he was mocking me.

"Eustace, come…" I drew him down amidst my heap of cushions. "War is over. Duke Robert is deposed and my sire is the new Duke. Our position in Normandy is stronger than ever. What could go wrong to vex us?"

"Aye, what could go wrong?" He grasped my waist, pushing me down into the nest of pillows, his anger forgotten, and it would seem, his weariness too.

Later, when he lay snoring beside me, arms akimbo, wiry body red in the glow of the beeswax candles set in cups around the chamber, I lifted my arm and gazed once more at Eustace's gift. The beaten copper band, pecked out with intricate patterns, faintly mirrored my worried face, distorting my features until my visage hardly seemed my own but a long, warped mask about to break apart as the mouth gaped open in a silent scream…

CHAPTER SIX

The next year, I gave birth to another daughter, Peronelle—Little Peter. She was indeed my small 'rock' to shield me when I was buffeted by Eustace's storms; I would creep to the nursery and hold her, wishing I could feed her instead of the wetnurse—but to do so would be most inappropriate for a lady of my rank. I could only stroke her silken reddish hair and smell the soft milk scent of her, and sing the little bedtime songs I had learned as a child in England.

Eustace's moods were increasingly foul and descended on him with no warning, leaving those in the path of his anger terrified and often reeling from blows, but at least he was often away—Father had rewarded him with several more castles, which he fared to while on long progresses. I hoped these new properties would satisfy him, but no, it seemed not. He never forgot Ivry, worrying at the thought of it as a terrier worries a rat, and for some reason, after appropriating it from Robert, Father had decided to hold onto that particular fortress, bestowing it on none of his favourites and leaving it in charge of a loyal castellan.

"My ancestors owned that castle—it was a gift from the Duke at the time!" Eustace would grumble, digging his knife into the tabletop or a window ledge as if he wished he were truly thrusting it into Father's heart. "It was wrong of your Father to seize it back after removing Curthose from his dukedom. He should remember the meaning of a gift."

"Those kinds of gifts are not like other gifts—you should know that, Eustace," I told him. "They can be taken back at any time if the Duke or King thinks it fitting. You have Breteuil and Pacy and four other stout fortresses. What is so exceptional about Ivry that you must constantly fret over it?"

He could not answer and looked cross that I had asked. Yes, Ivry's walls were thick, its design unusual, but there were richer domains and castles just as stalwart which he legally owned. The truth was, it was being told he could not have it that inflamed my husband's childish desire to have it as his own.

The King often returned to Normandy on business. He made all efforts to tie England and the Duchy together, leaving advisors and justiciars to dispense law when he was absent. To further encourage strong alliances, a whole bevvy of my illegitimate half-sisters was married to various lords and princes; we children of Henry were dotted about Europe like pieces on a vast chessboard. One half-sister, Sybilla, the daughter of Sybil Corbet, one of Father's favourite paramours, even married a King—Alexander of Scotland. I wondered what kind of husband a Scotsman might make as opposed to a Norman lord.

The year after that, old Philip, King of France, died and his son, Louis, took the throne. He was of a vastly different character to his sire and immediately began making outrageous demands of my Father. He commanded the return of Gisors, a strategic fortress taken after the battle of Tinchebrai, while insisting that Father was his vassal and must bend the knee to him in homage.

The King was furious and sailed across the Narrow Sea with an army, seeking, once again, to assert his right. Sometime after his arrival, I met with him at Perche. Eustace had gone off to his castle of Pacy, siting 'business', which filled my being with concern, for I thought it was unwise not to show open loyalty to the Duke of Normandy.

Tilda was there to greet me, still pretty but sad-eyed, with her two fair daughters. Little Felicia was still small and frail, walking with a slight almost imperceptible limp, but at least, beyond all hope, she had lived through the most dangerous phase of childhood. Our half-brother, William Adelin, was also in the welcoming party, having come over from England, not to fight, as he was still just a little boy, but to witness the doings of Kings in preparation for his future life as a ruler.

He had grown into a tall, sturdy boy, ruddy-faced and with sparkling, intense blue eyes. Tilda seemed to have fallen in love with our young half-brother; she fawned on him, had many gifts brought to bring him pleasure—ponies, puppies, marble chessboards, books, jugglers and jongleurs. I imagined she perhaps saw him in some wise as the son she had never borne. I thought of my William, back with his nurses in Breteuil, and was grateful for him. Even if Eustace was distant, travelling upon his own dangerous path, my son was there, my crowning accomplishment—the heir to Breteuil, Pacy and our other castles.

"Sister Juliane!" Young William Adelin turned to me. Tilda had been trying to teach him a courtly dance but he was, like so many lads his age, all ungainly legs, and he had stepped on her toes and tripped on her gown. He was amiable in personality, though, and did not storm angrily or whine despite his failure on the dance floor. "Sister Tilda said you have many hawks at Breteuil. Did you bring any with you? I should like to see them."

"Oh, please, my Lord William, none of this 'sister' business, I beg you!" I stood before him, looking down at the bright head below. "You make Tilda and I sound like a pair of withered old nuns."

Tilda put her hand to her mouth and suppressed a small laugh; it was good to see her mirthful for once. William Adelin blushed. "I did not mean to cause offence."

"I was not offended at all," I assured him, "but we need not use such formal terms here. Just call me Juliane—not Lady, not Countess, not Madam…and not Sister, either And I am sorry but no hawk—I left Breteuil in haste and travelled lightly."

William Adelin looked crestfallen.

"I do have a fine hound, though, who journeyed with me. I am sure you will like her; she is as white as snow with two black patches, one over either eye. I will introduce you later and you can take her for a walk in the castle bailey."

The thought seemed to cheer him and he grinned. "I have many fine and kindly sisters, my Lady…I mean, Juliane. You are all much kinder than Adelaide."

I blinked. "And what does Adelaide do that is so unkind?"

"She teases me constantly. She is very fierce and will kick and punch even if she is threatened with a beating afterwards. She says she has the heart and temperament of a King, not I, and therefore she should sit on the throne instead. Is that not a wicked thing for a girl to say?"

"Extremely wicked," I said, hiding a smile. It seemed my little half-sister was cut from the same cloth as me, for good or for ill.

William had the more even, sunny temper of his mother, Queen Matilda.

Our conversation came to a close as King Henry entered the chamber. Silence descended and we all curtseyed or bowed in the royal presence. Father, who had spent the day hunting in the forest with Count Rotrou, wore a hideous black scowl. Had the hunt not gone well? Had he fallen from his horse or missed bringing down a stag?

My gaze fell on his clenched fist; he was carrying a scroll, crunched up in his iron grip. Wax from a broken seal sprinkled the parchment like flecks of blood. Bad news, then.

"Gather round, gather round!" he shouted, his face florid above the raven jut of his beard. "I want you all to hear a tale of infamy."

I put my hand on the young Prince's shoulder. "William, I think we should go. Tilda, shall we leave?"

Ever keen-eared, Father overheard my whisper. "No, no, Juliane—stay. Matilda, too, and the boy. He must learn about treacheries and disasters, for that is the lot of Kings, to deal with such infamy!"

He threw himself down at a table, casting off his thick fur cloak, like some bear from a childhood tale shedding its skin to become a man. Squires and pages swirled around his royal person, bearing flagons of drink, bringing food on trenchers. Once the drink was in his hand, Henry downed it in one great, slurping draught, then looked over to his knights and barons, and to his startled and uncomfortable family.

"News has come and it is not good news!" His voice emerged, a low growl in his chest. For a moment, he made no other move, just sat with lowering brow and black visage. Then, suddenly, his infamous rage erupted. Leaping up with a wordless shout, he flung his goblet across the chamber. It struck the wall and bounced off with a clang, showering cabochons torn from its rim. He then kicked the table over, spilling platters and ewers over the floor. He grabbed his seat and hurled it away, taking his cloak with it. To everyone's horror, the cloak landed on an edge of the firepit, where it began to smoulder and let off the terrible stink of burning fur. Squires rushed to drag it forth and stamp upon the little flames that greedily licked the edges.

The sight of his expensive garment in ruins might have heightened his wrath but, mercifully, it seemed to cool it. With a grunt that was half a groan of misery, he grabbed his bench and hauled it back upright, sitting heavily upon it, his back bent, his head lowered.

"Father?" asked Tilda tremulously, stepping towards him. "I fear for you. I beg you tell us what has happened."

The King raised his head, his expression bitter. "You know how hard it has been for me to keep hold of Normandy since I imprisoned my brother Robert. Well, King Louis, God rot the imp, threw his support behind the brat, my nephew William Clito, along with Fulk of Anjou."

"Yes," said Tilda, unusually brave, "that is well known. But it is all over now, surely, is it not? In the end, most men of wisdom saw that a child-ruler would be nought but a pawn in the hands of ambitious men, and so they accepted that your claim was just and true."

Father sighed. "They did…but, alas, daughter, it is never so simple as that. You would not understand. Men's hearts are fickle…"

"And yet it is women who are often accused of fickleness!" I blurted, then blushed furiously, fearing I might have aroused his wrath yet again with my over-eager tongue.

Instead, I raised a weak, weary smile from the King. "My Juliane, ever fierce, the defender of her sex…" He shifted uncomfortably on his seat. "Anyway, the news I received is about William Clito himself. After Tinchebrai, I was kind to the boy and left him in the household of Count Helias and his wife, who was Robert's daughter. However, when I recently asked that Clito be handed into my keeping, Helias's castellan and steward made excuses why he could not be: Helias and his lady-wife were not in residence so they dared not obey me for fear of their master's punishment…the boy had the sniffles and must rest…there was plague in the castle, felling anyone who breathed in the rancid air."

His fists clenched dangerously, his temper rising again. Purple stained his cheeks, an unhealthy glow that hinted of apoplexy, the killer of irascible older men. "Well, now I have received news that the bastards have smuggled the brat out of Normandy—he is now hidden somewhere in Flanders where I cannot get hold of him."

Secretly I was rather relieved my little cousin was far away—he might be a dangerous child, but he was still but a child—although, of course, I did not want him used as a weapon against the King.

"I would blind the little shite, if I had hold of him," Father snarled, eyes narrowed and hot with wrath. "That would stop anyone wishing to put him up as a puppet-ruler!"

I shuddered; I knew the King was famed for his rages but was not familiar enough with him to have heard him utter such words of violence.

"You will go after him then, my liege?" Rotrou Count of Perche stumbled forward, his face the colour of old cheese. Former crusader though he was, he had been enjoying the peace of his existence in Perche—breeding horses, growing grapes for wine, enjoying the fruits of the lands of Belleme, which had annexed upon that evil lord's downfall. "War will be declared on the Counts of Flanders?"

Henry sat back, hands splayed on his knees. I watched them, calloused, sprinkled with tough black hairs, hands that had caressed my mother Ansfrida, hands that had cradled his baby bastard daughter tenderly so long ago. Hands that wielded the sword in battle—the sword of justice and sword of vengeance both. Hands that itched to get hold of a terrified young lad and blind him.

The room swirled dizzily around me and I clutched at Tilda's sleeve in distress. She held my hand; both of us felt the other tremble, the cold sweat of each other's palms. If there was war, both our families would find themselves dragged into the heart of it.

The King was silent awhile, gazing at all our pale faces, then shook his head. "No, let the boy stay where he is. I shan't waste good soldiers chasing William Clito into Flanders. Not worth it. When he is grown, let him face me as a man and we'll see who is master of Normandy then, eh?"

A sigh of relief passed throughout the chamber. Father looked vexed for a moment at the reticence of his retainers to leap into battle on his behalf, then, to everyone's relief, his shoulders slumped, the fury in him dying.

"Pah, it is always the same, my whole life fighting for what is rightfully mine," he grumbled. "I must not let it get the best of me—

although I suspect it will be so until they bury me in my grave. I must dwell more on the happy news, the new alliances made…"

"Yes, yes," Tilda broke in, falsely over-cheerful as she tried to improve his uncertain temper. "Happy tidings are what we must hear, not evil ones! Tidings such as our sister Sybilla marrying King Alexander of the Scots. Imagine, an alliance between England and Scotland."

"Yes, imagine," said Father dryly, as if he knew full well that it would not take long before the Scots were at loggerheads with him once more, despite the glittering marriage of Sybilla to their King. "However, more alliances are to be made; this is true. There is one small light in the darkness of these days…" He raised his head, a faint, satisfied expression on his features. "My legitimate daughter, Princess Adelaide, is now betrothed to Henry V, Emperor of Germany. A fine match, I am sure you will all agree."

Affirmative mutters went through the chamber. All I could think of was how young Adelaide was—and the Emperor was at least twenty years her senior. Still, hers was the fate of women of high birth—no choice in the matter of a husband. It might not prove so bad in the end; stranger matches had turned out successful, even harmonious. And then there were marriages such as mine, which had begun with promise but faded into a state of cold, bored endurance, punctuated by small episodes full of either angry recriminations or strained tolerance.

"I am sure Adelaide will make a mighty Queen," I murmured, thinking how our brother, William Adelin, had called her 'fierce.'

"Better a dutiful wife than a termagant, but I'd expect no other statement from a wildling such as you, Juliane!" said Father, but he was laughing now, honestly, the storm of rage past.

"Let us drink and eat," said Tilda, desperate to keep the day on an even keel. "And minstrels—where are the minstrels? We must have music!" She clapped her slender white hands and a stream of musicians stumbled into the Hall, having been hidden in waiting behind some curtains. They looked flushed and jittery, no doubt having heard the King's furious outburst, and began to play with almost wild abandon, the crumhorns wailing, the bagpipe squealing, the tabor beating out of time.

It was a strange ending to a strange day.

Soon I headed home to Breteuil again, eager to see Lora, Peronelle and William—while hoping that Eustace was still at Pacy on his supposed business.

All I could think of, as my chariot bounced over the rutted roads, was the flushed wrathfulness of my Father's face—and his talk of putting out the eyes of his young nephew, William Clito. The thought nauseated me, as did the swaying of the carriage; I would almost have thought I might be pregnant by the churning in my gut, but there was no chance of that. My couplings with Eustace had dwindled to almost non-existence in the last little while.

I tried to sleep, to pass the journey and quiet my mind, but it did not work. Every time I closed my eyes, I saw a child's face, the eye-holes open and weeping both blood and tears, and above it, filled with determination, dagger in hand, my sire, the King of England.

CHAPTER SEVEN

Fractious as ever, the Norman nobility began to rise against their Duke in ever-swelling numbers, many clamouring for William Clito or for the return of his father, Curthose, which Father swore would never happen as long as he had breath in his body. I feared if the Norman lords clamoured and caused trouble much longer, Uncle Robert, locked away in the fastness of Devizes, might find *himself* without breath in his body. Robert de Belleme, emerging from whatever evil hold he had crept away to, was foremost among the rebels, despite his reputation—if there was one man I wished Father *would* slay, it was the Devil.

Eustace journeyed back and forth between Breteuil and his other five castles. On rare occasions I travelled with him, usually when Breteuil Castle needed a clean-out—the privies flushed into the lake, the rush matting taken forth and burnt on pyres that sent up clouds of rank smoke into the sky. Sometimes I even travelled with my daughters—only the girls, for Eustace would not allow me to take William, his shining jewel and only son—accompanied by my ladies-in-waiting, who fussed and fretted over the children as if they were tiny, jewel-clad dolls. Even old Gundrada, who occasionally wandered in her wits these days and imagined she was a young girl back in England, came with me on occasion, riding in a litter.

It was on my own, however, that I journeyed to Father's court at Bonneville. Tilda was there and several half-sisters of whom I knew but little—Constance, who was wed to Roscelin de Beaumont, Aline, wife of Matthieu de Montmorency, and one of the many Matildas, this one married to Conan Duke of Brittany. To my delight, however, I found that my brother Richard had crossed the Channel to visit his father's Norman court. I had not realised he was present until I spotted him in the tiltyard, showing off with sword and mace against a chosen adversary from amongst Father's best knights, while William Adelin stood on the sidelines with his tutors, yelling encouragement while virtually dancing with excitement at the prospect of battle between the two combatants.

"Richard!" In my surprise at seeing my brother, my tongue was loosed and I called his name. Equally surprised, he half-turned and lost his footing—his opponent clouted him heavily on his helmet and he fell to the ground like a pole-axed ox.

"Richard!" My cry of shock now became a scream. Pushing Idonea and Cecelie aside, I raced towards the fallen form of my brother. He lay flat out on his back, arms and legs akimbo, his blade fallen to churned-up ground.

His sparring partner, a young man with curly red hair, had removed his helm and was staring down at Richard in shock. "I did not mean to hit him so hard. We train together all the time. Usually, he's nimble as a deer…"

Richard uttered a groan and his eyelids fluttered. Groggily, he strove to sit. I fell to my knees beside him, uncaring that my lovely gold-threaded green dress was now smeared with mud.

"Richard, are you hurt? Shall I call for a physician?"

He blinked up at me, pulled his helmet off and chucked it aside. "Is this an angel come to bear me away to heaven? Or is it my sister Juliane come to torment me?"

"Richard, this is no joke. I fear for you; he hit you so hard…"

"I'll have a nasty headache tomorrow, I fear, and a few bruises to mar my good looks but nothing more… Don't fret so; it makes you sound like Mama." He began struggling to his feet. The red-headed fellow helped him; Richard leaned heavily on his shoulder as he rose. "Despite the circumstances—It is good to see you, Juliane."

"Oh, you too…you too, Richard. Let us depart to somewhere quiet so that we may talk and reminisce in private! There is so much to talk about!"

"Let me get this mail off." He pointed to his chest. Mud oozed through the metal rings of his shirt. "I reek like a wallowing pig! I crave a bath to remove the stink and ease my bruises. But later, later this afternoon—the garden?"

"The garden it is," I said, feeling happier than I had for some time.

The castle of Bonneville was ancient, built of old by the great Charlemagne. My grandsire the Conqueror had favoured it greatly, and it was within its ring of stern walls that Harold swore to uphold William's claim to England. Of late, its wooden donjon had been replaced by five great stone towers and its ditches deepened; Father had added in small herb gardens and arbours to lighten the fortress' bleakness.

In a little knot of herbs and roses, I waited for Richard, anxious, in case he'd been drawn aside by Father for some other mission. But no, as the Nones bell struck in the nearby village, he appeared, walking a little stiffly, clade in a loose blue tunic to the knee, his black hair, worn longer in the English manner, waving around the white stem of his neck.

I went to him and we embraced, and for a while tears fell. He wiped them away with his thumb, looking concerned. "Are you not happy, Juliane?" he asked. "I always assumed it went well with you. Three living children…"

"My children are my joy," I said, "but my husband Eustace not so much. Not anymore. Oh…I feel disloyal for saying so, and he could be far worse, but still…"

"Ah," said Richard, colouring slightly, not knowing what to say.

I forced a smile. "How is Mama, Richard? And Fulk?"

"Mother is fine; she does not see the King anymore but she is content. She has found religion, would you believe."

I was startled. "You think she might become a nun?"

"I wouldn't go that far. But an oblate, maybe. Who knows? As for Fulk, he has no interest in anything to do with the King's court. He's become a successful merchant with no help from anyone, and is married with a huge brood. You'd hardly recognise him, Juliane. He is bald, would you believe!" He touched his own thick mop of hair in mock-horror.

"Bald so young! Poor Fulk." I stifled a laugh. I had a hard time imagining my rough, freckle-faced brother without hair. How the years changed us all. I wondered if Richard looked at me and saw a stolid matron far removed from the boisterous young girl of long ago.

"And what about you?" I asked him. "Surely you are wed by now? You're well past the usual age."

He shook his head, flushing a little across his high cheekbones. "I've escaped that noose—for now!"

"Noose!" My eyebrows lifted. "Richard! Marriage is the proper estate for good men and women according to the will of God!" I tried to look stern but a grin slowly split my face, unseemly but all too honest. "I must admit, however, sometimes it can *seem* like a noose."

"I will not escape matrimony for much longer, I do know that much," said Richard cheerily. "I believe Father has a worthy maiden lined up for me, Amice, daughter of Raoul de Gael. Father may be a hard man to please at times but I am ever grateful for what he has done for me, overlooking my illegitimate state. He ensured I had the best education possible from Robert Bloet, the Bishop of Lincoln, and he has seen that I learned the warrior's art from the finest arms-masters. I've been appointed as special guardian to our young brother, Prince William, which is why I am here in Normandy. Father wants Will to learn of statecraft from a tender age; and he says it won't hurt me to learn it too, for he wants me as William's right-hand man. One day, who knows…the King might raise my status to that of Earl or…" He shrugged.

"Oh, Richard, it is a great honour to tutor the Prince. And I am sure one day you will have an earldom."

He folded his arms. "I enjoy my duties teaching our little half-brother, but the job carries many responsibilities. And worries. Trust the wrong man, and one's head might end up on a spike above a town gate somewhere."

He began to pace; flower petals torn from the rose bushes in the breeze eddied around him, blood-red. "An envoy is coming from the French King, Juliane. He should arrive at Bonneville within the next day or two."

"What does he hope for?" I brushed a torn petal from my veil.

"The release of Robert Curthose."

"It will never happen. Father would die first."

"That's what his adversaries are hoping," said Richard dryly. "However, they have sent the foulest of men to try to strike a bargain, no doubt bearing threats of continued raiding if they do not get what Louis of France demand. Father's sworn enemy in England and now an ally to his foe—Robert de Belleme."

A gasp escaped my lips. I had tried to blot that evil-doer's existence from my mind. Long had he haunted my nightmares around the time when I lost my baby, Ralph, but with time's passage his malevolent presence had swept away like a withering ghost, leaving me in peace. Now, he was coming here to Bonneville. *The Devil.*

"You seem distressed." Richard caught my hand. "You have had dealings with this Belleme?"

"Only once," I said. "It was more than enough."

Richard folded his arms. "Well, sister, do not look so afraid. You need not fear him here. Master Robert of Belleme is going to get a nasty surprise."

Perhaps I should not have been there. Most women would have scurried away and hidden in their chambers, intent on their boring embroidery and prayers. I was not as other women. As much as I loathed Robert de Belleme, feared him—yet I wanted to see the great comeuppance Richard promised. Belleme had brought trouble to all and sundry for too long. His downfall would be my delight.

Father sat in the Great Hall of Bonneville castle upon a high dais, covered by a canopy of silver stars and golden lions. He wore his crown and a robe that poured like molten gold around his ankles. I was seated on the benches to his left, partly shielded by a screen, but I could still see what was taking place. Richard and William Adelin were on the opposite side to me, amidst a great crowd of noblemen and churchmen loyal to Father—and a throng of hulking, sullen-faced knights in mail, clearly ready for trouble.

A horn blared, its sound almost a belch, brassy and flat. I noticed Father's back straighten and his eyes glitter as the vast doors at the end of the Hall glided open and a black-mantled figure strode toward him, surrounded by the toadies of King Louis arrayed in the gaudy colours associated with the Capetian kings.

"Halt!" Father raised a hand. "No closer."

The delegation halted. Robert de Belleme gazed haughtily down the Hall. "My Lord, I am here as an emissary of his Grace, King Louis of France. Will you not hear my word, as is the custom?"

"Oh, yes, yes, Robert," said the King testily. "I know what the custom is. Let's hear what Louis the Fat plans to harangue me with now."

Belleme approached the dais slowly, a shadow, a spider, that white, strangely still face a frozen mask under his dark headgear. My heart hammered, despite myself. He could not hurt me here, in this strong castle, near the high seat of my own sire, the King. Yet if he were truly the Devil's Own, a sorcerer... Cold sweat began to roll down the back of my neck beneath my fine linen wimple.

Belleme positioned himself before the King, legs spread apart in a gesture of pure arrogance. Reaching beneath his cloak, he yanked out a parchment scroll, opening it with an exaggerated flourish. "His Grace King Louis of France asks the following of Henry of England—that he remember he be vassal to France, and that he release the rightful Duke of Normandy, Robert Curthose, from imprisonment and see said Duke is restored to his lands and position, and that the heir of Robert's body, William Clito, is given safe passage into his sire's lands, and given assurances that when the time comes, he will assume his father's titles and properties without impediment or interference from said Henry."

Father made a snorting noise. "Doesn't ask for much, does he? What's he going to do if...*when* I refuse?"

Belleme's chin lifted; his little eyes narrowed to slits. "He will make war, my lord King. Already barons flock to rise against you. Normandy will burn from the inside and then France will arrive to finish it—and you—forever. Your imprisonment of Duke Robert is lawless—give him up, before all turn against your illegal rule and you lose not only Normandy but England, and..." He shrugged rudely, leaving the threat hanging in the air. The warriors in the Hall loyal to Henry muttered in anger at his presumption.

Father shook his head, irritated rather than dismayed or shocked by his bold words. "Robert...Robert, when were you ever a true friend to my brother? Or anyone. Oh, maybe my other brother, William Rufus, God assoil him—oh, not that he'd approve of me saying that...not God. I know you two loved raiding abbeys and the like—and Christ knows what else you got up to together..."

There was a dark murmur of laughter from around the vast chamber. My Uncle Rufus was known as a sodomite, who disliked women both in the bedchamber and as persons. He had at one time considered wedding Matilda, who later became Father's Queen, and even visited her in the convent where was living with her Aunt Christina, but he could not bring himself to do so, not even for the sake of the succession. I am sure Matilda, pious and decent, was greatly relieved...

I peered beyond the edge of the screen for a better view of Belleme's face. My father's mockery had given him a little flush to his pallid, drawn features, the first I had ever seen on that emotionless visage. I wanted to laugh but had no wish to draw that creature's malignant attention to my presence.

"So..." Belleme waved the open parchment in his hand. "Enough of these idiotic japes and jibes. What is your answer to King Louis?"

"You know it, Robert de Belleme. No."

"I shall depart then, forthwith..."

Father leaned forward in his seat, and now he was smiling but it was not a friendly smile, rather a wolfish, predatory one. "Oh, no you won't, my wily friend..."

Belleme flung King Louis' missive to the ground and took a step backwards. He had no weapon since only the guards were allowed to carry them in the Hall, but his hands were curled into fists and he looked like a wildcat ready to spring. "Do not be a fool, my Lord King. You dare not harm me!"

"I'm not going to harm you...much. Guards!" He beckoned to the men lined up behind his seat. "Take him and bind him in chains. Put him in the dungeon and then ready him for a journey to England."

"You cannot do this!" Belleme roared. "I am an emissary of the French King, I act for him and am his mouth—in this capacity, I *am* him!"

"I will stopper that mouth, and I'd do the same to Louis the Fat," said Henry. "I have heard enough! *Guards!*" Soldiers clanked forward, spears and swords at the ready.

Belleme's expression was more furious than frightened. "This is an outrage! It shows you for the tyrant you are! Not only do you assail an ambassador from another King, contrary to all rules and decency, but you also imprison me without charge!"

Father held up a hand. "Not without charge, my lord of Belleme. Here, squire, bring me my documents!" A young lad ran forward, holding a long strip of parchment. "Here are the charges. I prepared the list before you arrived."

The King cleared his throat and stood in all his majesty, the torches flaring behind his crowned head, the firelight flickering on his golden robe and the jewels he wore on neck and hands. "Firstly, you are accused of failure to attend your Duke and King at court, despite being summoned three times. Secondly, you have refused in the past to render your accounts unto me upon request. Lastly, you have acted against your sworn lord's interests and now serve an enemy King, which is treason. There—do you want me to go on, Robert? This could take all day…"

Robert de Belleme's thin lips writhed like worms. I thought for an instant his bestial nature might take hold and cause him to spit in Father's direction. However, he did not do so, but as the soldiers laid hold of him, pressing the tips of their weapons into his flesh and roughly binding his arms behind his back, he laughed, an odd, deep, throaty sound under such circumstances.

He fixed Father with that infamous unblinking serpent's gaze, and said steadily, "You have got what you long wished for, after first robbing me of my earldom and my castles. Now you rob me of my freedom. Yet it will not always go so well for you, Henry Beauclerc, I foresee this…" His voice dropped to a menacing hiss. "You have many bastards but only one son. One son. So easy for death to creep in, for waves of darkness to swallow all hopes…"

Instinctively, I pressed my hands to my ears. He was the Devil's son and it seemed to me he prophesied death to my family. I saw others around the Hall cross themselves in shock. At my back,, I could hear someone reciting Our Lord's Prayer: *"Deliver me from evil…"*

Father, however, appeared undisturbed by Belleme's outburst. "Get this loathsome creature out of my sight," he said to his guards, and they hustled the black-clad nobleman away to Bonneville's noisome dungeons.

Later, I met with Richard and William Adelin in the solar. "So, the Lord de Belleme got his just desserts at last, Juliane," said Richard. "You need not fear him more. Indeed, all of us can now sleep better in our beds."

"I have heard he has a son, though," I said cautiously.

"Aye, but he favours his mother and she was no lover of her husband. I believe he will behave."

"I wish Father had cut off the evil man's head!" said William, full of flushed, youthful exuberance. "I would have if I were King."

Richard frowned down at our little half-brother, the circlet denoting his princely rank shining on his parted, deep-gold hair. "Now, William, there is a lesson here—you must learn to temper justice with mercy. As King, you will also have to make decisions that follow the laws you have made, even if they are not popular."

"Even if those laws, in the end, hurt those you love? Even if it means wicked Belleme escapes death and breaks free to trouble us again?"

"Even then, William."

William's small face became solemn and he blinked up at Richard with huge blue eyes. "Being King must be so hard. Sometimes…it must hurt Father to do what he must do."

"Sometimes, but not this time," said Richard. "Robert de Belleme is a bad man. Not bad enough for the axe, under the law, but bad."

I went to my chamber and my ladies frothed about me, commenting on what had happened in the Great Hall while they readied me for bed. As I sank down beneath the coverlet, I thought of Belleme, locked far below with the rats, the slime and the dripping water. His final words before his incarceration had chilled me when he spoke them but I knew I had nothing to fear from him now.

Oddly, what lingered in my mind were the childish words of Prince William, spoken in all innocence—*It must hurt Father to do what he must do.*

CHAPTER EIGHT

I returned to Breteuil. Glad in heart, I rushed into the garden to find my little daughters playing amid the flowers, chasing butterflies through the purple sprays of lavender while their nurses watched them with beaming faces. Lora was bending over, her golden hair a shining halo, as she smelt a rose; Peronelle, still very small, was teetering along behind her, her mouth in a gap-toothed smile, her long white robes fluttering like the wings of the insects she chased but never managed to catch in her chubby baby hands.

When the girls caught sight of me, they shrieked with excitement and rushed to my side. It was perhaps not the dignified greeting they should have been taught to give, even at their young ages, but I had no care for that as I scooped them up, one under either arm. I was so glad to be back, after all the intrigues of Court.

"William fell in the moat!" Lora suddenly announced. "He was fishing!"

My heart lurched and guilt filled me. I'd rushed straight for my daughters and neglected to seek out my son—the all-important boy, Eustace's heir. And now Lora was telling me an accident had befallen him...

"Mama, why are you so pale?" Lora toyed with the glass beads of my necklace. "William is not hurt—other than his rump. His tutor has beaten him for not taking good care! He is not allowed to leave the nursery for a week!"

I breathed a sigh of relief and buried my face in her long, golden hair. I fancied its smelt of sunshine. "Well, I guess we had best go see him and cheer him up in his 'imprisonment'," I said. My voice wobbled a little.

"Papa's already there!" said Lora. "He came last night."

I hesitated. Earlier I had noticed Eustace's banners displayed above the turrets. The thought of meeting with him did not fill me with much gladness but I had to make an effort for my children's sake—and because it was what a dutiful wife should do. At least that what the priests said.

I put Lora and Peronelle down on their feet and beckoned to their nurses to collect them. "I will let your Papa have some time alone with William and will not pry on their meeting. As for you two little hoydens, you two must go indoors now with your nurses; it is nearly time for Mass."

Later in the day, after the children were all in bed, Eustace came into my solar. Hastily I dismissed Cecelie and Idonea, who shuffled out with heads bowed, looking very chaste and downcast. I suspected that within several minutes all propriety would be forgotten and their ears pressed to the closed door.

The scent of alcohol clung to my husband but, mercifully, he was sober if baggy-eyed, his chin blue with stubble. He had also grown a little red moustache that I instantly loathed.

"So…you've decided to return, Juliane," he muttered, not altogether friendly.

"How could you even think I would not?" I said. "I was only visiting my Father's Court; my brother Richard was there—I have not seen him for years!"

"Our son fell in the moat."

"So I heard. Boys do such things. I trust his nether regions were well-whipped over such folly."

"He could have drowned!" Eustace's eyes bulged.

"But he did not!"

"Christ, woman, you should have been here, watching over him. He is my only son!"

"It is not my duty to watch him every waking moment—I am a noblewoman, of the blood royal, not a peasant in the field. I have other duties—and it is prudent to keep on Father's good side. He certainly wondered where *you* were and what you were up to! And as for me leaving Breteuil to go to Bonneville, well, you were off at Pacy!"

"Doing *things*!" he roared.

"Like what, ruminating about how to take hold of Ivry?"

He waved his finger threateningly under my nose. "You go too far; you have always gone too far."

"Put me aside then," I said, and in my moment of anger, I truly meant it.

To my surprise, his face crumpled; he raked his hands through his hair. "How has it come to this—this endless bickering. We were good together once. I do not want to seek an annulment."

"What *is* it you do want from me?"

Suddenly he grasped my hand and kissed it. "Another son. A boy to replace poor Ralph. A man needs more than one son. Maybe you do not understand that as a woman. When I am old, who will help to protect my lands, my castles? William…William is…"

"William is what?" I said defensively.

"A good boy," he finished, rather lamely, "but have you not noticed, he has not grown as much as the other castle boys. He sometimes…*wheezes* when it is cold. He looks younger than his age; I would not wish to send him to another lord's household for training, as is the usual way. He is too precious. Too frail."

My face crumpled. I had noticed but had striven to ignore it—not because I did not care but because I did. And the thought of losing him to some childhood malady terrified me. Admitting his frailty would have made it all too real. And to think I had once pitied Tilda because her daughter Felicia was sickly. My boy was little different.

I put my hands to my face. "I—I feel I have failed you utterly."

"Do not…he will probably grow out of this stage, but a second, or third, son would bring added security to my position. Do you understand?"

"I do," I said, getting hold of my emotions "but if we are to revive our marriage to what it should be, you must understand me too. No more yearning for Ivry; it will bring no good to either of us. I also expect no anger if I should wish to visit Tilda or Father; they are my family and we owe the King much. Never forget that, Eustace. Never."

"I have been harsh. I have dwelt in bad company." His shoulders hunched up, furrows crossed his brow. It was hard for him to admit he had committed any wrong-doing—but he attempted it, which I appreciated. "I will try…to be more loyal, both to you, my Lady Wife, and to King Henry."

"Do you swear it?"

"I swear!"

"Will you promise one more thing, husband?"

"Whatever you wish, Juliane. Let me try to make amends."

"Tomorrow, call in the barber. Get rid of that moustache."

He stared at me in shock—and there was an abrupt flash of anger in his eyes. Then he slapped his hand on his knee and began to laugh. I started to laugh too, muffling the sound on my sleeve in case he grew angry that I laughed too loud at his expense.

"It is a deal, wife," he said, reaching forward to kiss me, first on forehead, then upon the lips. "It is a deal!"

So it was that we made peace with each other, of sorts. I suspected Eustace had grown slightly worried about his unwarranted absences from Father's Court after hearing about the fate of Robert de Belleme. He wondered what I had said about his behaviour and if any action would be taken by the King. I had said nothing unfavourable, save to Richard in private, but if Eustace's fear made him shy away from his unsavoury friends and show some attentiveness to me again, I certainly would not complain.

Together we rode between our six castles, sometimes with the children, sometimes only with our attendants, and we managed our lands as a good lord and lady should, settling disputes, curbing rowdy knights who oppressed the farmers who tilled the land, making sure the crops were in on time and the tithes paid. The second son Eustace wanted did not materialise, alas, but he never broached the subject again; who could argue with the will of God in such matters?

Good news arrived that the King had met with Louis of France at the disputed castle of Gisors, and the French King decided to allow Father to hold all the fortresses on the borders of Normandy. The threat of war with France dwindled and so too did the grumbling and threats from many of the Norman barons, now that Father manned all the great strongholds, filling them with fierce, loyal men-at-arms and sure-sighted archers.

Father was jubilant and proceeded on to the wedding of my sister Adelaide to the Emperor of Germany. She had already been living in Germany for several years, cared for by Bruno, the Archbishop of Trier, and had been crowned Queen of the Romans in the city of Mainz. Her name was changed to Matilda, which the

Germans deemed more fitting than her birth-given name; the old Adelaide was gone forever and a new little Empress took her place, from all accounts haughtier and more straight-spoken than most women thrice her age.

In January, when snow blanketed Germany, she finally left Bishop Bruno's household and was wed to Emperor Henry in the cathedral at Worms before a glittering host of dignitaries, while the ordinary folk celebrated in the streets, dancing upon the snow, roasting beasts on spits, decking themselves in winter greenery till they looked like wildmen of the woods.

No sooner had the wedding passed, however, than Father had to return in haste to the shores of Britain; the Norman lords in Wales were under attack from the Welsh princes whose domains they had taken in warfare. It was a trying time, for Wales was a dark and dangerous land, filled with wild streams and high bleak hills and mountains, and the people there spoke a secret, ancient tongue outsiders found impossible to learn. The Welsh were also fierce, proud people and eager to regain the kingdoms they had lost.

But once again, God smiled on Father's endeavours and he prevailed against his enemies, and the rebel leaders, Gruffyd and Owain, were forced to sue for peace. It meant, though, that Father would remain absent from Normandy for a while, while he made certain the peace in Wales and the Marches would hold.

It was Richard who rode to Breteuil to inform me that Father was returning to Bonneville and that my presence, and Eustace's, would be required at Court.

"You've ridden all the way to summon me yourself?" I asked as I sat facing him in Breteuil's Great Hall, wolfing down great chunks of bread dipped in steaming gravy—simple fare, but what he desired most to quell the hunger from the long road. "Why not send a courier?"

"Father wanted me to impress upon you...or rather, your husband, that you both must attend. It is very important. We shan't be staying at court for long; we will together fare throughout Normandy, on a royal progress. We must impress the populace, and show harmony and cohesion."

"Harmony and cohesion in Normandy. It will never happen," I said wryly.

"Do not jest, Juliane. This is important—for our brother William's sake."

"For William? How so?"

"Father plans for him to become the Duke of Normandy in the future, as you might imagine. Unfortunately, even though his rule has been just, and the malice of troublemakers such as Belleme has been quelled, many men still rally to the cause of Uncle Robert's son, William Clito. They truly believe he is the rightful heir."

"He is not even in the country."

"No, this is true. He bides with enemies of Normandy. And recently the King found out that when William fled Helias' castle, he went straight to Belleme's fortress before faring on to Burgundy with his supporters. I fear Clito will stir up a nest of bees; the old, warring, enemy lords of Belleme's affinity—and his own sire's."

"So, what does Father hope to do?"

"Show the people of this land that we are a family united. That William Adelin's rule would bring peace while William Clito's would bring endless war. He must bring the future Duke to the common folk and make them love him."

"Do you think such a plan would work?" I said dubiously. What good would come of pacifying the commons?" It was the nobles who were the problem. From what I could see, the noblemen of Normandy thrived on fighting and reiving. They were, after all, the descendants of the Northmen, of whom the Saxon scholar Alcuin had written in his chronicles, quoting the words of Jeremiah, "*Then the Lord said unto me, Out of the North an evil shall break forth upon all the inhabitants of the land.*"

"It must work," said Richard, face anxious and strained. "Otherwise, we lose hold of Normandy. And if we lose hold of Normandy to William Clito, many of us will find our lands and livelihoods forfeit. We will end up driven across the Narrow Sea back to England—and then William will come for that too, as our grandsire did long ago."

We fared to Bonneville, the whole family, Eustace riding sullenly beside an excited Will who sat high in the saddle upon a docile piebald mare we had given him on his nativity day. Lora and Peronelle, clad in identical dresses of blue silk with embroidered red flowers along the cuffs, neckline and hem, bounced around inside the chariot they shared with me and their nurses. The women chided them, trying to keep the peace, and glanced helplessly at me when they could not. I ignored the ruckus around me; it amused me to see my daughters so rambunctious and decided to let them be, this once— for I knew such frivolity could not go on forever. They would be young ladies soon enough, demure and soft-spoken, eyes downcast, their voices moderated and pleasant to appeal to prospective husbands…

Reaching Father's fortress, we crossed the busy bailey and climbed the tall wooden stairs into the Keep, where the Chamberlain led us into the King's presence. He was just heaving himself out of a great wooden bathtub, attended by his squires; he was completely shameless and unembarrassed, a huge bristly boar of a man, and I glanced at the floor, flushed, glad my children had been spirited away to the nursery.

Standing before us, dripping water, his hair slicked down on his skull, he beckoned for the squires to rub him dry. They wrapped him in a great piece of woolly cloth and began to rub madly, their faces reddened with the strain. "So, you've heeded my summons," he said, jovial in tone though with a small bite in his words. He gazed straight at Eustace, dark eyes piercing, his intensity making my husband shift nervously from one foot to the other.

"Your Grace, there was no chance we would not…"

"Well, I am glad to hear that, Eudo…"

Eustace started. "Eudo? Highness, I am Eustace…"

"Oh, aye, aye," smirked Father, shrugging into a saffron silk tunic. "Foolish me. I forgot your name for a moment. I see you so rarely…"

Eustace's cheeks flamed and he mumbled apologies that seemed, to me, to worsen the situation. Father looked smug, enjoying his discomfiture. "Well, Eustace…" He clapped my husband on the shoulder, a mighty blow that almost sent him reeling against the bathing tub. "Make sure such long absence does not happen again, eh? I am sure you would not wish your loyalty to ever be in question."

"N-no, my liege," Eustace stammered, and he fell to one knee in the puddles on the floor.

"Good man." The King leaned over him, water dripping from his beard onto the crown of his son-in-law's head. "Now, come, Juliane, you must show me my little granddaughters and grandson. I am eager to see them."

He reached for my arm and together we left his bath-chamber. I glanced over my shoulder. Eustace was still kneeling, head bowed in contrition, in a spreading pool of water…

The royal party set out across Normandy. The King rode at the fore, his lion banner flaring, another lion leaping, red-clawed, from his surcoat of imported silk. William Adelin accompanied him, clad all in gold, a headpiece that looked suspiciously like a ducal coronet upon his shining fair hair. Behind the prince fared my brother Richard, mentor and teacher, and all the great lords who supported Henry, mounted on their war-horses, the pennants carrying the insignias of their Houses crackling in the brisk wind. Minor retainers followed, under their own banners, and then all my half-sisters and their children came in carriages or brightly-garlanded litters. In the rear of the cavalcade marched stout soldiers and a contingent of archers, in the event of any trouble.

I shared a chariot with Tilda and her girls, Philippa and Felicia. Both had grown into very pretty maids, even though Felicia had never quite outgrown the frailty of her early childhood and held her belly as if the rollicking of the carriage would make her spew. I hoped Tilda had told the nursemaids to bring a bowl in the event her daughter should be sick.

All through the countryside we journeyed, like a band of itinerant players, which is what we sounded like, only on a grand scale, for Father had paid for multitudes of musicians to play on the edges of the procession. Hordes of people turned up to view the party as it passed by, from mud-daubed peasants and goodwives in grubby wimples, to wealthy shopkeepers and merchants, to black-clad nuns flocked together like crows and burly monks in their brown cassocks, whose tonsured heads sweated as they pretended not to cast lusty glances at the nuns.

And with every step along the way, young William Adelin attempted to charm them, smiling at winsome young women, waving his hand at the ugliest toothless crone or scowling bondsman. He certainly looked the part of a prince, even though he was only twelve. He seemed older since he held the promise of great height in maturity, and he clearly had been taught well in his duties as the son of a King.

Beside me, Tilda sighed; the day was hot and the chariot humid—she sipped watered-down wine from a small, silvered chalice. Are you well, Tilda?" I asked. "You do not look happy."

She glanced towards her daughters and mine; all but Peronelle had fallen asleep in the heat. Peronelle was leaning with her head on the ledge of the window-slit, trying to breathe in some cooler air from outside. Her bronzed curls stuck to her flushed brow.

"I am well, Juliane, but I fear this is all show, all mummery. It will do no good."

"What do you mean?" I fanned myself with my hand. Beads of sweat were breaking on my brow.

"Did you not see their faces, out in the street? The people here are set in their ways. Uncle Robert was their Duke, and it seems they liked him. It does not matter how many good works Father performs for their benefit; he is seen as a usurper. Our poor brother, William; he is too young to see it, but I am not—they laugh at him in his gold, as if he were but a frivolous popinjay—or, worse, they give looks that savour of malice. They will not have him, not without war. They want instead a lad they have never seen, who is growing up far away, for the simple reason his Father is *not* Henry."

I sat back on my tasselled cushion, pondering my sister's words. Could her fears be true? Jesu, the land would lie blood-stained for years.

Across from me, my pale little niece Felicia finally succumbed to the rolling of the carriage and the excessive warmth of the day—and was noisily sick onto the floor.

The end of the progress came with huge thunderstorms that broke the intense heat. If one thought that might prove a good thing, one would be wrong. Lightning flared like God's wrath unleashed and thunder shook the earth, frightening the horses in the entourage and making them difficult—and dangerous—to control. The chariot I travelled in was pulled this way and that until Father called for a halt and we all took shelter in a sad little town, where suspicious faces glared from ramshackle stone houses and a half-ruined castle, a single defensive tower with a crumbling wall, frowned from the top of the hill.

Seeking shelter from the castellan, we abandoned the panicked horses and began a march on foot up the incline, the Bishops and clergy parading before us in their ecclesiastical robes, attempting to give our arrival some form of dignity.

Rain gushed down, pounding our exposed heads, lashing into our faces. Water funnelled down the slope, running like a small river around our ankles, ruining our shoes, staining the hems of the women's gowns. The children were shuddering and shivering, slipping on the mud; Tilda picked up Felicia as any peasant-woman might do and I did the same with Peronelle. The nurses dealt with the other children, holding their hands tightly to keep them from falling.

Up ahead, I could see William Adelin's back as he trudged through the muddy deluge. He tried to remain proud and upright, but his golden garb dangled on him like a wet sack, darkened by the water, and his coronet hung askew on sodden hair. He walked stiffly, slowly, the mud making embarrassing sucking noises as it dragged at his legs.

Suddenly he lurched forward; his expensive gold-buckled boot had come off and remained encased in the mud while he hopped helplessly on one foot.

From amidst the thin lines of townsfolk clustered on the roadside braving the rain, there came a loud bray of laughter. Then another. And another.

Striding next to William, Father looked as thunderous as the sky. For a moment, I feared he might shout for the soldiers to fall upon the insolent, laughing locals with their swords. But he did not.

"Onward!" he growled, pointing up the hill, "but when this storm ceases, we are returning home. This folly is *finished*!"

CHAPTER NINE

Back in Breteuil, life went on. And death. Old Gundrada finally passed into God's keeping; a mercy really, for she had become like a child, gibbering and singing to herself, talking to members of her long-dead family. I wept more than most thought seemly for a lady of my rank but she had been part of my life for so many years, the last tie to my bygone youth in England. I had her buried in the local church beneath a fine marble slab that Eustace resented paying for.

After the disastrous tour of the country with William Adelin, Eustace's temperament had soured yet again. He had not liked Father's constant jibes and moaned all the time that he was unappreciative of such a good son-in-law. He began to neglect me and never spoke more of producing another son; I suspected he might have other women, although I dared not pry. On top of it, he had a new friend with whom he spent much time, hawking, riding, and I daresay bombarding with his woes, a man my sire hated—Amaury de Montfort, Count of Evreux.

Amaury was the son of Simon de Montfort and Agnes de Evreux; he had gained his title through his childless maternal uncle. Father had attempted to stop his accession to his lands and held him away from them for nigh-in six months—but in the end, the constable of Amaury's castle let de Montfort in when Father was on business in Rouen. De Montfort's family were notorious, particularly his sister, Bertrade; she was a long-time mistress of the old King Phillip of France but had managed to convince him to wed her—despite the fact both were still married to others at the time. Even threats of excommunication did not halt their sinful plans. Later, rumours abounded that Bertrade sought to use sorcery to kill the young Louis, Phillip's heir from his first marriage, so that her own son would one day rule France. If true, it clearly did not work and she ended up taking the veil in Fontevraud—and Amaury, well, he became an avid supporter of Louis.

The Bible says that Lucifer was the Light-Bearer and beautiful, and that was how I saw Amaury. A man of middling height, he had uncannily handsome features along with thick, curling brown hair and flashing white teeth. A man fair to gaze upon but wicked to the core, corrupt, whispering tempting words in Eustace's ear just as the Serpent in the Garden whispered to Eve, making my husband even more dissatisfied with his lot, making him wish for more…making him wish for Ivry.

Yes, the question of the castle of Ivry came up again. It loomed, dark and threatening, in the back of my mind. Such an odd thing too, that Amaury should fill Eustace's mind with new thoughts of claiming the castle. Once upon a time, the de Montforts had tried to claim it too but failed. I knew not what Amaury's motives were but, in my heart, I knew they were evil ones.

Many a night I would watch Eustace drink himself insensible with Amaury egging him on, a goblet in his hand too, yet nearly always managing to remain mysteriously sober. "I cannot bear it," he moaned one evening after he had dined with his new companion. "My castle Ivry with Ralph Harenc as Castellan, sitting in the high seat, lording it over all when he is but a nobody."

"Outrageous." Amaury leaned on his elbow across the table, a little smile playing on his handsome features. *A mocking smile*, I thought. "A man of your stature should not have to put up with it."

"My father-in-law the Duke hates me, loathes me, likes to see me squirm!"

Amaury sighed theatrically, all the while letting his gaze drift in my direction, knowing his words would offend, yet uncaring. Savouring his insolence, even. "Henry of England did the same to me, my friend. Kept me from my own lands, which were inherited from my dear Uncle. That is one reason why I support King Louis. He has ever been a fair, just man."

Sitting at the side of the Hall beneath the window with Cecelie and Idonea, I felt like taking my embroidery needle and stabbing the vain knave to the heart. My maids, shocked by de Montfort's open insult to the King, shook their heads and tutted in low voices. I gave Eustace a meaningful glance, a warning that such talk was not welcome, but he ignored me—as he often did nowadays—and merely poured himself and Amaury another drink.

It was I who left the Hall, both angry and ashamed, feeling an outsider in my own home. As I left, supported by my maids, I felt

116

Amaury's taunting gaze fixed upon my back and a great, intense fear enveloped me, a fear I had never before experienced. The torches blurred and my ears started to ring. Gasping, I ran ahead of my maids and burst out into the gardens. Outside, the chill night air struck my face, chasing away the evil humours that possessed me. Leaning against the base of one of the towers, I inhaled the night-scents of the flowers, the smell of the rich, dew-laden earth. Above the stars winked, hard white eyes watching from the vastness of God's firmament.

A sense of my own helplessness flooded my heart.

Evil was coming. I felt it with every fibre of my being.

Father was embattled. King Louis threatened invasion once more, along with his allies, the Count of Anjou and the Count of Flanders. Eustace sweated and fumed, fearful that he would be called to swell the King's army with his levies. Amaury continued to whisper in Eustace's ear, words that inflamed my husband's desire for that wretched castle at Ivry.

"Let him know that you will support him only if you are given what is rightfully yours," he said lazily. "You are no longer a youth, Eustace; it is time he respected you as the man you are!"

What kind of man was he? There were times I thought I knew him not at all. We had always blown hot, then cold, like the winds that shrilled across the castle on its high rock, but this time it was different. He was sunk in self-pity, twisted by the greed fuelled by his false friend—and steeped in wine until he smelt like a brewery.

In May, though, I had more to worry about than my husband's drunkenness and poor choice of friends. A messenger arrived wearing Father's livery; ignoring Eustace, which put him in high dudgeon, he asked to speak to me in private. Weariness made him stagger; his face was wan. Dust from the road hung in his throat; his voice emerged a harsh croak.

With Eustace glowering at my back, I took the man aside into my solar, saw that he was given ale and a stool to sit upon; he was clearly fatigued, scarcely able to remain on his feet. "My Lady," he said. "I come bearing ill news. Soon it must be told to all across Normandy but within this castle, I would tell you first."

A sick wave of fear passed over me but I held my emotions in check as I had been raised to do. *Father*...I thought, *it must be Father. He is ill...or worse...*

"Tell me, messenger," I said. "Do not hold back. No harm will come to you, no matter what tidings you bear."

He took a deep breath and suddenly tears glimmered in his eyes. "My Lady, there is no easy way to say it, for forgive me—but her Grace, Queen Matilda, is dead."

I gasped, my hand flying to my mouth. Matilda was not of my blood but she was of my family, and my Queen. How clearly I remembered her kindnesses in Winchester; her gentle smiles, her plump cheeks and thick white-gold hair, reminders of her Saxon heritage.

"It was unexpected. She caught a fever, perhaps from the waters of the Thames while travelling on her barge, and died at the Palace of Westminster. Already people speak of her as a saint, just like her mother, the Blessed Margaret. Long will men remember her holiness; how she walked to church bare-footed at Lent, how she founded hospitals for the lepers, how she washed the feet of the poor and held the hands of the sick to her lips to give them of her grace."

Tears started to stain my own cheeks. "How will my Father the King manage?" I said. For all his chasing of women, Matilda was his rock, loved by the people, a calm island amidst a rough sea. "I dare say...he must return to England at once." The gravity of my own words hit me. If he left Normandy, the county would lie wide open to invasion by Louis, even with the King's mightiest captains in charge. Some might interpret Henry's departure as craven flight or, without his continued presence, turn their coats and go over to Louis...

"My Lady, if I may be so bold as to say so, I believe his Grace will act decisively and in the only way he can."

"And what do you think is that way?"

"Although he wears mourning garb and prays for the soul of the blessed Queen, he will proceed to harry the French and their allies. He will not return to England. His Highness the Prince William is there to oversee the burial arrangements, and good men such as Roger of Salisbury."

Yes, the messenger was right. Father would not leave Normandy in peril, not even to arrange the funeral in Westminster of his faithful Queen. A King did not attend the burial of his consort besides; it was considered inappropriate for a crowned head.

I called out for a money-chest and paid the courier well for his sad tale. Then, taking a deep breath, I went out to tell Eustace.

When I told him, he crossed himself but a strange expression flickered across his face. It was uncharitable, but I thought my husband looked furtive, like a rat. He had something in mind and I easily deduced that 'something' was unsavoury. It was also something he would not share with me...

The King was coming to Breteuil. Despite all the skirmishes and uprisings across Normandy, despite renewed treachery and incursions into his lands by King Louis, he was taking time to ride to the castle and talk to Eustace.

Now I knew why Eustace's expression had borne a slyness when told of the Queen's death. While Father was grieving for his wife, while his thoughts were consumed with plans for defeating the French and quelling rebellion, Eustace would do what he had always desired to do—write to the King and ask him outright to be given the castle of Ivry. With his 'polite request' to assume the property of his forefathers was a small but obvious threat—that if he did not get what he craved, he might not find himself able to assist with any future military endeavours, being otherwise occupied in his role as seigneur. Amaury de Montfort, hovering over his shoulder like a gore-crow over a dead carcass, convinced him to even add a little more to his letter, implying that he thought that perhaps King Louis was not altogether a bad fellow to have as a friend...

I was horrified and heartsick when I heard that Eustace's presumptuous, insolent missive had gone out to Father, but Eustace and Amaury, deep in their cups, guffawed and bragged about it like a pair of idiotic beardless youths.

"Ivry will soon be mine!" Eustace chortled, munching on roundels of salted wild boar between gulps of wine. "I'll throw that bastard Ralph Harenc out onto his arse and drive him off with a whip if he protests!"

"Harenc is a foolish, sour-faced oaf," nodded Amaury, smiling, handsome—and, this time, also very drunk, perhaps feeling victorious now that Eustace had finally been persuaded to act the brazen fool toward his father-in-law. "He must be pried off that castle as one scrapes a barnacle from the hull of a ship."

"Does one scrape barnacles off ships?" Eustace asked, quizzically, drunkenly, as he slumped in his chair with wine-stains down his front.

"I know not..." slurred Amaury, "but we can certainly scrape away unworthy villeins from positions they never should have had in the first place. Why, you'd think Ralph Harenc actually *owned* Ivry, the way he behaves!"

"Father owns Ivry." Unable to listen to any more foolishness, I suddenly stood up, cheeks blazing. "And there is doubtless a very good reason why he wants it to remain in his keeping."

"Yes!" Eustace's lower lip stuck forth like a pouty child's—I had seen the same expression on the children when they were chided. "I know what that reason is! To hold it over me that all I own comes from him, and that he can clutch onto my ancestral lands as long as he wants! Well, to do so is wrong. I will impress that fact upon him."

"Go carefully, husband," I said in a low, warning voice. "The King has a short temper and his rages are fearful. He has lost his Queen and trouble brews. If he suspects you of treason..."

"Ha!" Amaury banged his cup down on the table before him, making candlesticks and plates judder and jump. "What a bold and beauteous wife you have, Eustace! Telling her husband how to run his business! Lady..." he raised his goblet again, in a mocking salute, "I salute your courage."

My temper flared and I made to offer a violent retort but Eustace shook his head and flapped his hand in dismissal. "Go, my Lady. This is not the place for you if you cannot behave as a woman should and keep opinions to yourself. Go to the nursery, a more appropriate spot for a female to dwell."

"Well, the girls are certainly better companions of late than you, Eustace," I spat. "Although I dare say you hardly notice you even have two daughters. Do you even remember their names?"

He bridled in fury but before he could explode, I swept from the room, near running down the corridors and up a flight of spiral stairs to reach the children's chamber.

Dismissing the startled nursemaids, I knelt by the bedside of my dear little daughters, both fast asleep. Burying my hot face in Lora's long, sun-golden curls, I wept with fear, frustration and distress.

Father was baggy-eyed and greyer than I remembered. Dismounting stiffly from his great war-horse, he lumbered like a bear into the hall and thudded down on a carven chair beneath a jewelled canopy. His mouth was a long, tight line, his eyes black below beetling brows. I sensed the anger in him, subdued at present but not far from the surface.

I curtseyed and made to voice my sorrow at the death of the Queen, but he shook his head curtly and motioned me aside with a brisk wave of his hand. "Not now, Juliane. I must deal with this accursed business of Ivry."

Curtseying again, I back away and retired to my place with my ladies and Lora, Peronelle and William, whom I had brought into the chamber to see their royal grandfather—and to, hopefully, temper his mood with their presence.

"Well, Eustace," said the King, "let us make this as swift as possible. You have drawn me away from pressing business. It seems you think your personal wants are greater than the security of the Duchy of Normandy."

Eustace shifted uneasily; Amaury was nowhere to be seen, a wise thing on his part since Henry loathed him, and he was not so confident without his overbearing friend. "Your Grace, the lordship of Ivry has long dwelt in my mind. However, the time to speak to you was never right."

"And you think the right moment is *now* when we are in the midst of war?" Father's brows shot up, bristling.

Eustace coughed and spluttered for a second or two, then an obstinate expression gripped his face. "It is exactly the right time, my Lord King. A time when men must decide where they stand and for whom."

My stomach churned; why must he be such a fool? Beside me, William nervously stared up at my face; only a lad, and young for his age, but he sensed the tension in the room.

"So, it's like that, is it?" Father's hands gripped the sides of his seat until the knuckles whitened. "Your loyalty to me extends only as far as the gifts you are given!"

"No…" Eustace took a small step backwards, unnerved by the anger in the King's eyes, "but your Grace, Ivry is mine by right; my ancestors held it! I could protect those lands for you, raise armies to fight the French."

"You question the skills of my castellan, Ralph Harenc?" queried Father. "He has always served me loyally and looked after my castle well."

"He is not its rightful master!" spat Eustace, fists suddenly curling as if he would punch the air around him. "He is but a servant yet he sits in Ivry like a petty lord. He laughs at me; he thinks I am but a poor bastard who made good only through my marriage. I know he does."

"How do you know such a thing, Eustace of Breteuil? Who told you?"

Eustace's face was crimson. "Amaury de Montfort, Count of Evreux. He has heard such talk."

"Oh, has he? You are more of a fool than I thought if you've put your trust in that snake. An arse-licker of Louis the Fat." Father's lips curled contemptuously. "Well, if you have a problem with Harenc, I have summoned him here to Breteuil. You may tell your grievances to his face."

Eustace's flushed countenance deepened to near-purple as a tall, spindly man stepped from amongst the King's party and stood before him. Harenc had a long, flat face, liverish-yellow, with a heavy fringe of black hair across a high, bony brow. His surname, oddly enough, meant 'herring,' and it was indeed a kipper-fish he resembled.

"Ralph Harenc, you have heard what Count Eustace claims you have done," said Father "Have you anything to say on the matter?"

"I do." Kipper-faced Harenc had a dry, flat voice. "I have indeed said that Count Eustace is no fit lord and should never hold a castle as important as Ivry."

A gasp went through the assembled nobles in the chamber. "You bastard—how dare you?" screamed Eustace and he flung himself toward the hated Ralph Harenc—only to have his arms grabbed by Father's guards, who hauled him back, struggling and cursing.

"I dare," said Ralph Harenc, and his little eyes, like two damp brown mushrooms, ignited with long-suppressed anger. "For I have many grievances against you."

"What are these grievances?" asked Father. "Do not fear to speak, Ralph. I will not favour the Count just because he has wed my daughter, Countess Juliane."

Harenc took a deep breath. "He has sent raiding parties on to my land, attacking villages, stealing and pillaging—he's no better than a reiver! He has stolen deer from my deer-park and fowl from the forest."

"You lie!" screamed Eustace, struggling against the men who held him.

"Then what is this?" Ralph Harenc held up a pewter badge. It was the livery badge of the men of Breteuil, a cross with a star and many flying eagles.

I groaned. Now I knew what Eustace had been up to with Amaury when they were away from Breteuil. Raiding the lands under Ralph Harenc's guardianship, trying to make him seem an incompetent castellan, unable to protect the villagers and uphold the Laws of Venison.

"It...it wasn't me," Eustace continued to bluster, despite the evidence before him. I could hear muffled snickering throughout the room—not all of it from the men one might have counted as enemies.

"If it was not you," said Father in an almost weary tone, "then it was your shifty friend, Amaury de Montfort, working on your behalf."

More protestations came from Eustace. More grappling with the soldiers, who held on all the more tightly, grim-faced.

The King held up a hand for peace. "I am sure a solution can be reached," he said. "One that may even please you, Eustace. Believe it or not, I have considered giving you Ivry as you have long wished."

My husband made a strangled noise and sagged forward in shock, his knees kept from hitting the flagstones only by the efforts of his gaolers, who shored him up "You…y..what?"

"Yes, I considered it, for the sake of my grandson, your son William, who I wish to see come into a decent inheritance one day. I could also use the services of Ralph Harenc elsewhere in Normandy in these troubled times. However, due to your pillaging and thievery, your lying and your bone-headed folly, I am not so certain…"

"My Lord King!" Eustace ripped out of the soldier's hands and flung himself on the floor at Father's feet. "I swear to you, I would be a good lord. A faithful lord. Ivry would flourish in a way that has never been seen before…"

"Stop grovelling, man." Father frowned, pursing his lips in irritation. "After your revolting behaviour in Ralph's domain, I must think some more on whether I want you to have Ivry or not. I have more on my mind than your petty wants."

Eustace grasped the hem of the King's robe and pressed it to his lips. "My liege, all I ask is that you consider my claim!"

"I will consider it…in good time," said Henry with a smile that suddenly made me feel cold inside. "Until then, a way must be found to keep the peace between you and Ralph Harenc, No more raids from you and Montfort; no more insults from Harenc. There must be hostages."

My mouth went dry with fear. Hostages! Who could possibly fill that role? Eustace had no brothers or sisters or…

"Ralph…" Father had turned to Harenc. "You've brought your son, haven't you, as I ordered? Nice, intelligent boy—age what? Nine or ten?"

"Nine, your Grace," said the castellan, "but Roger is tall, as I was at his age."

"He shall stay at Breteuil as surety for your good behaviour these coming months. To make certain Count Eustace of Breteuil also behaves himself and will not harry your lands, I will in return take as hostage…" He paused, thinking, his dark eyes unreadable.

A sick fear overwhelmed me, making my heart hammer. No, not William, not my boy. He was my only son, Eustace's pride and joy, his lawful heir. He was not a healthy boy; all could see that by his thin shoulders and drawn face. He would become sick away from Briteuil and his nurses, maybe even die…This plan was wicked, preposterous…

"…I will take my two granddaughters, Lady Lora and Lady Peronelle."

A scream rose inside me; the chamber whirled. The carved angels on the roofbeams seemed to fly, their ash-smudged faces mocking. The girls—he wanted to take my girls!

On his knees on the floor, Eustace was still scrabbling about, fawning over the edge of Father's robe. "Yes, your Grace, I will agree to this hostage exchange. Thank you, I thank you for considering my claim to Ivry after so many long years."

"No!" The word burst from my lips, although it was impertinent for a woman to intrude on these matters. "You shan't take my daughters as hostages. They are not much more than babes."

Exasperated, Father glared at me. "I should have asked you be removed from the room," he said testily. "I might have guessed you would object. Do not be foolish, Juliane. It is the only way to ensure peace and co-operation. It won't be forever—a few months, a year at most."

I puffed like a bellows, head muzzy, still spinning from shock and the effects of my ragged, swift breathing. "A year! I cannot bear it. Nor can I bear the thoughts of my poor children locked in that gloomy castle with that…that fish-faced man!" I flapped my hand at Ralph Harenc, who looked truly shocked by my outburst.

Father heaved himself up. He was not a tall man but he had great presence that made him seem a veritable giant. "It will be done," he said. "You need not fear, Juliane—I have no plans to let my granddaughters go to Ivry and 'that fish-faced man' as you put it. They will come to court and receive the best of care. I want to get to know these children; soon I will need to think of fitting marriages for them."

"Father, I beg you…reconsider. I will offer myself as a hostage instead."

"Do not be foolish; you are a countess and needed to run Breteuil while Eustace is occupied elsewhere. Besides, Eustace has already given his permission for the girls to be hostages. He is their father; they are his property, to do with as he wills."

My tongue trembled, clove to the roof of my mouth. I could not speak; there was nought more I could say. I gazed at Eustace, crouched on the floor like a dog, and wanted to kick him. He had given my children away—for a godforsaken castle!

Cecelie and Idonea rushed to my side, murmuring words of solace, supporting me with their bodies as I staggered like a drunkard. I struck at them, trying to push them away, but they gripped my arms and propelled me from the hall and toward my bedchamber.

Once inside, I fell upon the bed in wild paroxysms of weeping. When I had finished, red-eyed and half-crazed, I leapt up and flew past my ladies-in-waiting and wrenched the door of the chamber open. A guard stood in the corridor outside wearing the King's badge.

"Let me pass, damn you!" I screamed, trying to jostle past the man, who blocked my passage with the butt of a spear.

"I am here on King's orders, milady," he said.

"Am I a prisoner in my own home?" I shouted.

"No, milady. His Grace fears you might harm yourself in your distress. Hence he wants you protected."

"Protected! *Protected! The lying bastard!*" I sank to my knees on the freezing floor and the tears gushed forth again, streaming down my face.

Idonea emerged from my bedchamber and helped me rise. "Please rest, Lady. This helps nothing, not you and not Lora and Peronelle. Please."

Hobbling like an old woman, I went with her and hurled myself on the bed again, face pressed into the coverlet. I would not speak, would not move, my hands gripping the fine fabric as if I would rend it to shreds.

At length, a knock sounded on the door and the king's own personal physician entered, a black-clad man with a long thin white beard. "I have brought a sleeping draught for you, my Lady Juliane."

Finally, I moved, sitting up with my hair mussed and my face a blotchy horror. "Sleeping draught? You might as well have brought poison!" I snarled.

"My Lady, will you not drink it?" said Idonea. "You will feel better when you have slept."

"Oh, give it me!" Rudely I snatched the flagon from the physician's hand and downed its rancid-tasting contents. "I care not."

Whatever the physician had given me, soon I was stretched on my bed in a stupor, possessed by evil dreams.

In the morning, shortly before dawn's light, my beautiful, loving girls, Lora and Peronelle, were bundled into a chariot and borne away to the King's court, hostages by the permission of their own selfish sire.

I was not even allowed to say farewell.

CHAPTER TEN

After the King's departure with his precious hostages in tow, I forced myself to cease grieving and do my duties as the Lady of Breteuil. Part of those duties was to see to the welfare of our new young charge, Roger Harenc, who was sequestered in the east tower away from our own son, William; indeed, away from the body of our household. This isolation was not my idea but that of Eustace, who could not abide anything to do with Ralph Harenc, but I was of a mind to see this setting apart ended. It would not do well for the child to complain of cruel handling, not with Lora and Peronelle as hostages at the King's court. Not that I thought Father would bring them harm but he might deprive them of privileges—and he might also deprive Eustace of lands, which would make him completely unbearable.

Silently I approached young Roger, who was sitting in his tower-room, reading from a prayer-book. He was a gangly lad, with bony knock-knees and the same long, sallow fish-face as his father. His shining cap of hair, however, was glossy black, and his eyes were large and down-turned at the corners, giving him a perennially sad look. Even so, he was slightly more pleasant of aspect than Ralph.

"Roger Harenc, I am Juliane, Countess of Breteuil." I smiled to gain his confidence.

Quickly he laid down the prayerbook, rose, and bowed. The bow was surprisingly courtly for one so young.

"I have come to find out if you are comfortable."

"Yes, my Lady." Roger's voice was nervous, a little wobbly. "Thank you for your concern, my Lady."

"You have enough food? You are warm enough?" I glanced around the chamber; its furnishings were sparse—*too sparse*, I thought—but the fire was burning in the brazier and an empty platter full of crumbs sat on the window-ledge.

Roger nodded gravely.

"I believe my husband, Lord Eustace, has employed a tutor?"

"Yes, my lady…or his Lordship has told me that he has. I have not yet seen the tutor yet, though."

"Is there anything else you require, Ralph?"

The boy's face twisted and I saw tears in his eyes. A lump knotted my own throat. "I would like to go home, my Lady, but I know that I can't. I must show courage for my father's sake."

"Yes, you must," I said, but although I pitied him, I would not hold out false hopes. "Do you have brothers at sisters at Ivry? A mother?"

"My mother is dead, Lady; she died not long after my birth. I do not remember her. I have two older brothers, John and Gui, but they do not live at home; they are in other households, receiving their knightly training. But I have many friends at Ivry—and that is what I fear most about dwelling here at Breteuil. I fear I shall be lonely."

I gazed at him, at his big imploring hound's eyes. "This tower is too far from the others," I said. "You are not a prisoner. I will have you moved into the nursery, now that my daughters have vacated it. I will introduce you to my son, William, and if you two like each other, and you show that you can be a good companion to him, I will let you play together at times. He is somewhat older than you, and yet...I think you might become friends."

His yellow, fishy little face lit up. "Thank you, my Lady Juliane. Thank you so much!"

Eustace was furious I had gone behind his back and moved Roger Harenc to the nursery but his fury paled before mine as once again I harangued him over what he had done to Lora and Peronelle. "Treat Harenc's child well! Remember that there are other children involved in this unsavoury matter—*your* children. Remember them? The ones you traded for a chance at obtaining a heap of stone. Maybe you care nothing for them because you think they are nought but worthless girls..."

"Enough, woman!" Eustace roared, pressing his hands to his head. "I can take no more of your sharp tongue! What's done is done!"

"Indeed, and I have moved Roger to the nursery, so that is done and over too. He stays there—he is a hostage, not a criminal to lock away in solitude."

Eustace glowered at me and stalked out of the solar. I heard him kick the wall. But I had won that battle—a small victory but at least a success.

Before long, William and Roger were playing draughts together in William's chamber. William said in private that he found Roger 'boring' but he liked having another boy around, even though Roger was some years younger; his words made me feel sad, for I knew he longed to emulate other of lads his age and status—and go to another household to learn the arts of war and horsemanship. But we could not risk it, not until he grew stronger.

Sometimes the two new friends ventured out into the bailey and I saw them shooting at butts and indulging in tomfoolery as young boys often do. It lifted my heart a little but my mind kept drifting back to my daughters. I told myself they would find themselves dazzled by the court and they would love Father showing them off to his courtiers like pampered princesses…but still I brooded over their absence.

At night especially, when shadows drew in and the castle slept, I would sit bolt upright, despite my weary eyes and aching limbs, feeling as though Death himself crept along through the corridors, calling, "*Juliane, Juliane! I am coming, coming.*"

Death did not come—but Amaury de Montfort did. With Father otherwise occupied with Louis' incursions into Normandy, he was back at my husband's side, companion of the drinking cup, teller of untrue tales, and an instigator of trouble, who could make a compliment seem like a slight and turn idle talk of treachery into a necessity.

I caught them in the hall, empty kegs around them, reeking of ale and wine and the horses they had ridden earlier in the day when they had raced each other like competing squires. One horse had fallen, its leg bending beneath it; the marshal had been forced to kill it with a blow to the head. Eustace had rolled free as the wounded beast crashed onto the ground, laughing in the manner of a loon, uncaring that he might have died for the sake of a game. He did not even seem to care that the horse had great value, its bloodline from Spain.

"You can get more horses!" Amaury had roared, clapping Eustace on the shoulder. "Buy some surer-footed ones next time. But, be that as it may, your misfortune, my friend, means that I have won the race—and you owe me a livre!"

Now, hours later, the two men were still on the subject of horses, but Amaury was slowly turning the talk towards Ivry. "I have my spies, you know," he was slurring. "They have fine horses in Ivry. Good grass there."

"Is that so?" said Eustace. "I'll enjoy adding them to my stock when the castle is mine."

Amaury shook his head. "Alas, it seems our friend Harenc has started moving them across country. He must truly fear the King will uphold your claim and is preparing to strip the castle bare of anything of value."

"Bastard!" growled Eustace. He flung back another mug of ale; he splashed himself in the face and the liquid fell onto his fine red tunic, making the dye run in bloody rivulets. "I am angered to hear this—I would say Harenc breaks the peace between us by such actions—Don't you, Amaury, my friend?"

The other man's face bore a look of such pretended sadness, I wanted to vomit. "I fear so, Eustace…and the horses are only the beginning of it. I've heard that chests full of money and goods were being removed under the cover of night."

"Might be his own, " grunted Eustace.

"Doubtful. How much wealth would a mere castellan have? No, I would swear on the Holy Rood, that he is taking any goods he fancies from the castle. His is embezzling coin from the treasury so that if you take on Ivry, you will be impoverished—and hence laughed at by the denizens of the region, who, for whatever reason, enjoy being under Harenc's oily thumb!"

"They must be lowly, ill-bred curs!"

"Indeed. But think of it, Eustace, if he is allowed to get away with his theft, what will happen if you take over and cannot pay your taxes to the King? You would not only look an utter fool, but Henry, I suspect, would be rather unforgiving. He might even strip you of the castle again, to make a show of you."

Eustace's teeth were gritted; his eyes sunken and red. "What would you counsel me, Amaury?"

"You should give Harenc a lesson he will never forget!" Amaury's visage lit up with perverse malice. To my eyes, he looked like some supernatural imp looming over my husband, his wild curls, reddened by the torchlight, almost seeming like tongues of hell-flame.

Eustace staggered to his feet, stood there swaying. Drink slopped again, froth flying everywhere, hissing as it hit logs in the firepit. His dogs, which had lain snoring near his feet, let out nervous yelps and shied away under a nearby trestle table.

"I will do it—I will show him!" he yelled, spittle flying from his mouth. "I will ride out to Ivry tonight and challenge him to single combat."

Dropping my embroidery, I turned around, ready to protest. I kept out of Eustace's foolishness as much as I could but what he suggested was preposterous in the extreme. And dangerous.

To my surprise, Amaury did not goad him on to ride madly into the night. He grasped his shoulder in a tight grip. His gaze, that sly, knowing gaze, slid over to me, teasing, tormenting, hiding his real purpose in the depths of his eyes. "No, no, Eustace; that is not the way to punish wicked Ralph Harenc. Is it, my Lady Juliane?"

"No, it is not the way," I said. "If there is punishment necessary, let the King deliver it."

"Ah, but he is so busy, Lady Juliane," said Amaury de Montfort. "We could not bother him with such petty little squabbles."

"Eustace, I think you should seek your chamber," I ignored Montfort and rounded on my husband, uncaring if I seemed like some ill-tempered fish-wife. "You are drunk. You can think on these matters tomorrow when your head has cleared."

Amaury snickered. "The good Countess tells you, Eustace…" he said mockingly. "So off you go like a good little pup." He made a series of silly barking noises.

"I'll do as I wish." Eustace glowered at me, eyes red. "*You* go to your chamber, Juliane. I do not know why you are down here anyway when you have your own solar. Typical female, busy-bodying and prying where she's not wanted."

Disgusted and increasingly angry, I picked up my skirts and beckoned to my scandalised ladies. "I shall leave, as you wish, husband; my head pounds from all your ravings. That does not, of course, change the fact that you still need to seek your own chambers—and sleep off your drunkenness."

Head held high, I moved towards the hall door. Behind me, I heard Amaury say to Eustace, "Let me tell you more about the treacherous Harenc. The things he continues to say about you—denigrating your lordship, your very manhood. He even brags of his virility in producing three thriving sons, when you have but one sickly one…"

I paused, glancing back in outrage at his slur; he smirked at me in that noisome way he had—a way in which, if accused of insult, he would look hurt and say you must have mistaken his intent.

Then he turned his back on me and continued to harangue Eustace, gazing intently into his eyes almost as if he were some odious catamite peering at a lover. "Ralph Harenc needs to be put in his place," he went on, ardent, intent. "Otherwise, even should Henry grant you Ivry, Harenc's loyal men will harry you and your coffers will lie empty. Men will laugh at you, call you an impotent churl, refuse to do their duty to their new lord. Listen to me when I tell you how, in my humble opinion, this should be done…"

Eustace swayed forward, clutching his friend's velvet sleeve. "Tell me, Amaury. Whatever you suggest to bring harm to my enemy, I will do!"

I faced away into the cool darkness of the corridor, grimacing with revulsion—and gripped with a growing sense of dread.

In the middle of the night, I was woken from a deep slumber by a thin, high, wailing noise. Rolling over on my side, I pushed down the covers. *There*…It came again, another thin wavering screech that was abruptly cut short. My breathing quickened.

Sitting up, I poked my bare foot at the shoulder of Idonea, who was lying beside my bed on her pallet, a rich quilt drawn over her. "Are you awake, Idonea?"

She mumbled something inaudible.

"Did you hear that…cry?"

"Yes, my Lady." Her voice was heavy with sleep. "Woke me."

"What do you think it was? Should I rouse the guard?"

"Cat probably," murmured Idonea, laying her head back down on the cushion. "It hasn't happened more than twice. All quiet now. Go back to your rest, Lady Juliane."

I lay back down, twisting the covers up around my shoulders. For some reason I still shivered, although it was not a cold night. For an indeterminate time, I sprawled on my back, unable to sleep, staring up at the black dome of the ceiling, but no more sounds came. Eventually, uneasy slumber claimed me. Once I half-woke shortly before dawn, when bluish light was creeping through cracks in the wooden window shutters, hearing the hooves of horses galloping. The sounds faded into the distance; the night-watch must have let someone pass, though to what end I had no clue. Messengers frequently came and went, mostly on business from Eustace's other holdings.

Frowning, I snuggled down into the warmth again and dreamed of a reunion with Lora and Peronelle. They were in a field of flowers, running, laughing, the wind free in their long hair, the sun above a burning gold coin in an endless expanse of blue. *Soon…it had to be soon…*

The day started ordinarily enough. Mass, then a walk upon the walls with Cecelie and Idonea, followed by a check on the buttery and a tally of supplies in the larder. Then a servant came, face crinkled in distress, bowing repeatedly before me. "My Lady," he said, "I know you are busy but, but I need to speak to you."

I recognised the man, Thierry; he helped out as a server at banquets and was also a carpenter in the town. "What is it, Thierry?" I asked, still doing my tallies of salted pork and dried fish and saffron. "Be swift. I am busy today."

"I found one of the little imported rugs you keep in the apartments—a Spanish one—thrown out in the bailey. It was lying rolled up outside by one of the towers."

"Really? How odd. Who could have done such a thing?"

"There's more, my Lady," he said nervously. "I unrolled it, and it was covered in blood."

I paused in what I was doing, alarm spiking through my being. "Blood?"

Thierry nodded. "It might have been that some servant passing through had a nosebleed and was too embarrassed to admit they ruined the rug, but I thought it best you were told."

I had begun to sweat. Cecelie was gazing at me with concern.

"Thank you, Thierry. You may go," I said. The servant bowed again and scuttled away into the bowels of the castle.

"My Lady?" said Idonea. "Do...do you think that scream last night..."

"No. It is likely nothing, an accident like Thierry thought...but I will find Eustace."

I went to the door of the larder, my ladies-in-waiting close on my heels. "No," I told them, stopping them as they made to cross out into the hall. "I must go to the Count alone."

I strode down the corridors, asking if anyone had seen Eustace. No one had. I sought out his quarters—nothing. His bed had not been slept in. I went to the Hall—there was nothing but the wreckage of his dining and drinking last night. I looked upon the flagstones; was there faint signs of cleaning? I bent low, touched a damp patch and inhaled deeply. Did I smell the faint iron tang of blood?

My stomach lurched; had Eustace fallen into fighting with Amaury? Had he hurt him, or had Amaury hurt him?

Whirling on my heel, I began to search the hall-block and outbuildings, asking the startled servants if they had seen their lord. No one had, not since last night.

As I searched in growing panic, I heard a voice calling my name. It was my son, William. He wore an expression of annoyance and puzzlement. "Mother, I am most upset..."

"William, I have no time for this," I said. "Go back to your rooms."

"But Mother, I was to play ball with Roger today, and then we were going to the kennels to see the new puppies. But I cannot find him. I've been to the nursery; he's not there."

My heart missed a beat. *Roger was not there...*

"Have you seen your Father? I am searching for your Father."

William nodded. "He is on the wall-walk. I don't think he is well, Mother."

Sending William back to the safety of his chamber, I hurried toward the walls, their stones tall and austere, throwing long shadows over the grass. Carefully I ascended the slippery steps leading upwards, trying not to trip—or to remember my terrifying plunge from the topmost tower, rearing over me like a black fist.

Reaching the top of the wall, I saw Eustace huddled in the shadow of a parapet, his cloak wrapped tightly around his body, his hood drawn up.

"Eustace!" I called. "What is wrong? Why are you up here? Where is Montfort?"

He thrust back his hood; his face was stark-white, the reddened eyes glittering feverishly—madly, I thought.

"Amaury has gone on a mission," he croaked.

"A mission? I do not understand. What mission? And where is Roger Harenc? William cannot find him; they were to meet today."

Eustace hesitated, licking dry lips; I noticed a smear of red on his cheek. "You…you've hurt yourself." I made to touch him but he shied away, snarling like a wounded animal.

"No, no, do not touch me, woman. Fear not, the blood is not mine."

"Amaury's?" I queried.

"No, not Amaury's."

I stood in sudden silence as I began to realise where the blood may have come from. "Where is Roger Harenc?" I repeated, my voice rising to a near-scream. "Tell me!"

"I have sent the whey-faced little brat back to his sire!" Eustace roared. "Sent him this morning with Amaury."

"Why…but why? And the blood…Is it his, Eustace? He…he…is alive, surely you haven't…"

"Of course he's alive!" Eustace raged, striking his fist against the side of the wall. Strips of skin tore away; his knuckles glistened crimson. "I am not a murderer."

"But you have done *something*; if you had just returned him to his father, you would not have blood upon you. You would not act in such a furtive manner, so secretive and strange!"

"I have done what needed to be done. Done what Amaury said I must do. Ralph Harenc stripped honour from me, took money from the coffers and made me sound an incompetent idiot to the people of Ivry. Well, I've made a fool of *him* now; I've stripped him of a healthy son…"

"But you said Roger was not dead!"

"Not dead—but mutilated. I have taken the boy's eyesight, Juliane. I have blinded Harenc's brat and sent him back to his bloody father."

CHAPTER ELEVEN

I galloped across Normandy like a madwoman, hurrying for the King's court at Bonneville. I rode astride in man's fashion, uncaring that the wind of my speed had torn the veil from my head and sent it spinning away across the countryside, allowing my hair to spill out in unseemly fashion before the eyes of all. Several soldiers from Breteuil thundered at my heels to protect me on the road—but Eustace was not amongst them.

Oh no, my husband, my foolish, brutal, easily-led husband had merely stared at me as I'd screamed and raged and begged that he come at once and ride to my Father to beg forgiveness for what he had done to Harenc's son.

"But why should I?" he had said, the drink still clearly hot in his veins. "It was for my honour, Juliane. Ralph had insulted my honour!"

"To hell with your precious honour!" I had cried back, weeping in both rage and terror. "You have mutilated a hostage, a young innocent boy. And the King has my daughters, taken for surety against evil behaviour from their father. He would be within his rights to harm the girls if he so wished!"

"But he will not do that." Eustace had grinned lopsidedly. "He's their grandfather. That's why I dared to blind the Harenc brat. Henry won't harm his own flesh and blood. He won't. Amaury said as much."

"You fool, you stupid, bloody fool!" I had lost my temper then and slapped him across the face as hard as I could.

He scarcely seemed to feel it and slumped back on the wall-walk. I thought he might have leapt up to strike me back but he had no strength left in him—and still too much wine coursing through his body.

Leaving him lying in a heap, I called to the Master of the Horse, who brought me a mount and bellowed for some guards to attend me on my urgent mission. Once they surrounded me, armed and in harness, I struck my spurs to the flanks of my swift mare and raced from the castle, down past the lake, through Breteuil town where the people stared and whispered, and then away toward distant Bonneville.

I *had* to reach Father before Ralph Harenc; I needed to throw myself upon his mercy, beg him for clemency, promise all sorts of things. Otherwise…who knows what action he would take? Maybe, maybe Eustace was right and he would not touch the girls, I told myself this, over and over again, but in my heart, I knew better than that. A cruel, stern idea of justice and fairness ruled strong in Henry of England; he would not weaken his position in Normandy by showing favouritism, even to his own family. If we had done wrong in Henry's eyes, we would pay a bitter price

But my girls, my innocent girls—they had done nothing wrong!

Roger Harenc, though, had been innocent too…

My horse died underneath me late that night, ridden until it could endure no more and its heart burst. Stopping in its tracks, lathered in foam and head hanging, it suddenly fell to its knees and started to roll over. Clumsily I managed to spring from the saddle to avoid being crushed, falling in a heap on the muddy roadside. Distressed, I began to pound the earth with my hands as rain lashed out of the midnight sky. "No, no, no…"

One of the soldiers approached me, stammering, "M-my Lady, you can take one of our horses."

I stared at their steeds, all nearly blown, froth on their lips. A few more miles of such hard riding and more horses would lie dead. I climbed to my feet, stiff and sore of body and heart. "No, there is no point," I said. "Let us find the nearest village and seek the comforts of an inn. I will try to purchase a new, fresh steed in the morning."

One of the men then dismounted and proffered me his mount for the short journey to a little village that stood on a smooth bald hill a mile or so away, the torch-light from the windows of its clustered timber-framed houses a welcome sight in the sodden night.

Reaching the village, my party continued down the cobbled street to the Inn, which was to my great relief half-empty. The innkeeper and his wife stared suspiciously at me as if I were the demon Lilith come to tempt them, and indeed, I likely looked like some type of night-hag flown in from the dark—my loose hair tangled with leaves and twigs, my face battered raw by rain and my clothing drenched. However, they cheered up when I brought out my purse to pay for a room in the inn for my use and lodgings in the barns for my men.

Once that was done, I retreated to the room at the top of the house, a cramped garret with musty hay on the floor and a chipped piss-pot in the corner. I took one soldier with me to guard the door. Stretching out on the grubby palliasse, I dragged a sheepskin over me and tried to sleep, but rest would not come. All I could think of was how Ralph Harenc would probably reach Father before I had the chance to please my case. How he would have raved of Eustace's cruelty, demanded justice, demanded retribution. *Retribution on my small daughters…*

Tears leaked from my eyes. I had tried but I knew I had failed my children.

The next morning my throat burned, fiery hot, and I shook with chills. Staggering into the common room, I summoned my men. "I will find a decent mount to purchase, then we shall be off again," I croaked, while they all looked doubtful, too afraid to argue but clearly unhappy with my decision.

Eager to show my resolve, I took a step towards the door. The room seemed to spin, while my ears started to ring and black specks floated in my vision. I slumped to the flagstones as the innkeeper's wife uttered a piercing shriek. The rushlights seemed to dance, dim, along the white-washed walls—then I knew nothing more.

I was sick for three days, unable to rise from the dirty bed in the attic room. I managed to eat some of the stew the innkeeper's wife brought me—for a steep price. It was dreadful muck, filled with the worst bits of offal and some tough chunks of turnip, but there was nothing better to be had.

I had given up my plans to ride to Father at Bonneville; the weather remained inclement and I was much too weak, so instead I had purchased a fleet young gelding and sent one of my men to deliver a missive to my Father, begging him for clemency in the matter of Eustace's sins. If my courier was swift enough, and he was a more skilful rider than I, he still might outstrip Ralph, who might not even have left Ivry for a few days while dealing with the shock of his son's mutilation. I had to cling on to that hope—and the hope that Father would wreak no evil on his own grandchildren.

Once I was up on my feet, I tottered weakly around the village, waiting for the response to my message. I could have returned to Breteuil but had no wish to see Eustace. So I wandered around the village pond, hissed at by the geese, pursued by hungry ducks and then walked downhill to the little market, where old dames in soiled wimples whispered about the identity of the 'fine lady.' I bought charms from a woman who might have been a witch; a dubious relic from a passing peddler; I chewed my nails down to the quick with the agony of waiting for news.

Then, at last, I spied my messenger riding at a brisk pace towards the village. He was accompanied by another rider; another messenger wearing the King's livery. It was this man, a tall and austere Norman knight with a scar from some old battle jagged on his cheek, who dismounted, bowed stiffly and handed me a sealed parchment.

My fingers scarcely worked as I broke through the wax seal, showering red flakes as if dollops of dried blood spilt from the parchment. Inside, the message was written by the hand of a scribe. There was no warmth, no cordiality, no tender greeting of father to daughter. *Countess de Breteuil*, it said, *Meet with us with all speed at our castle of Ivry. Impress upon the Count to join you; if he comes not, it is at his own peril. Be prepared to take back into your custody the infants as Ralph Harenc was given back his son.*

I folded the letter into the bosom of my travelling gown, uneasy at my father's final statement, but wondering if I read too much into his words. How else could he phrase my daughters' return? If Harenc had Ralph back, blind or not, the girls had to come home to us…

Queasy and sick to my belly, I galloped as fast as I could back to Breteuil. In the Hall, I found Eustace, alone, sitting at a table, staring into a bowl of coagulated soup and poking at it with a ladle. His eyes were glassy, staring, his face unshaven and his hair a greasy mess. It was evident he had been drinking again, although he appeared reasonably sober.

"Juliane!" he groaned, half-rising as I entered the chamber, supporting himself by one hand splayed out on the table. "What news?"

"This!" I cried and flung my Father's letter into his face. "We are to fare to Ivry without delay, and deal with the evil and dishonour you have brought upon our family!"

Ivry Castle loomed out of the morning mist, a dull, imposing grey block. Standing on a spur overlooking the sullen waters of the River Eure, I thought it one of the fiercest, most war-like castles I had ever seen—and I finally understood why Eustace craved it so, and why Father had shown reluctance to grant it to him.

A great ditch yawned before its stone walls, not filled with water but by fierce wooden stakes sharpened to keen points. A red-roofed guardhouse overlooked the narrow entrance, which was undoubtedly full of murder-holes through which defenders could pour hot oil and stinking waste gleaned from the latrines. Beyond that, reared the roofs of ornate apartments blocks and, over them, the fierce fang of the donjon, the Great Tower. It was almost twice as tall as ours at Breteuil, its walls an estimated ten-foot thick at least. Legend said it was once the stronghold of one Count Raoul, although built by the command of his wife, Aubree de Cachville, who then murdered Lanfred the architect, to keep him from building any other castle to the same plan. Later, Aubree was herself murdered—some said by an angry Raoul.

Thinking of my poor girls locked within, I shivered beneath my heavy travelling cloak. Soon they would be at home, where they belonged, safe within my care.

As we neared the gates, the flapping of banners assailed my ears; glancing up, I spotted Father's lions, gold and red against the misted heavens. The beasts' fangs seemed to bite at the sky, their claws to rip at God's firmament. At least we would not have to await the King's arrival; whatever punishment or deprivation he meted out to us would be delivered quickly.

The portcullis creaked upwards, gears and pulleys grinding. Riding beneath the gateway arch, I glanced up at those murder-holes I had mused on earlier, thinking how easy it would be for an enemy to kill us right now. Harenc was our enemy—but Father was not. Was he?

We guided our steeds across the bailey; grooms came to take our reins and lead the horses to the stables. Soldiers seemed to swarm around us like bees; both Father's and those of Ralph Harenc. Beyond were locals who worked in the kitchens and stables; loud booing went up as they laid eyes on Eustace. A rotten cabbage big as a man's head hurtled through the air, missing my husband by inches. Half of me wished it had struck him. At one time, he might have reacted with anger toward the peasants, even drawn sword in retaliation, but now he merely bowed his head and shuffled toward the steps leading up to the first floor of the mighty donjon.

Inside the castle, it was dark and rather rancid like most castles, smelling of men's sweat, unchanged rushes, smoke, and stale food. The passage was high, covered in ash from burning flambeaux; carvings of monsters and oval-eyed dogs leering down, their faces smeared greasy black.

We entered the Great Hall with no fanfare, no announcement such as we would usually expect.

The King was sitting on the dais, face as frowning as the side of a mountain. No smile split his lips; his eyes were flinty. It was as if Eustace and I were strangers, not family. The candles burning alongside him in a many-armed candelabrum cast weird shadows over his features, picking out deep furrows, funnelling darkness down from the end of his nose to his bearded chin. He reminded me of a craggy gargoyle, set high up on the tower of a church.

Unspeaking, he beckoned us forward with a curt motion of his hand. Eustace and I approached and knelt near his feet. I noted the floor below was mucky, rank; I dared not flinch, even when the stink of a dog-turd reached into my nostrils.

Still, the King did not speak; he just stared; his silence more awful than any words. My knees began to tremble; out of the corner of my vision, I saw Eustace's countenance grow mottled, red and white, awash with droplets of sweat. His hands were shaking.

Father glanced aside, off into a curtained-off area of the hall. He nodded to a squire who loped away. A few moments later Ralph Harenc appeared, his face ever tauter, sallower and more piscine that I remembered. As he caught sight of the kneeling Eustace, his lips curled in a sneer, then a snarl; he now resembled a wolf rather than a fish, one who would gladly tear out my husband's throat if he had the chance. Next to him, clutching his hand, was a child. His son, Roger. He wore a bandage that covered the upper half of his face and stumbled as he walked.

"This…" said Harenc, in a voice full of ill-controlled rage, "is my son, Roger. He was a healthy lad, of good mind and sound body. Till that man," he pointed an accusing finger at Eustace, "decided to maim him. He is now useless; he will have no trade, he will have no wife nor any children…" Poor little Roger flinched. "I shall send him to the monks, but there is little he can do even in a monastery. And this outrage was done not through any error of mine, but through the pure spite of Eustace de Breteuil!"

"Have you anything to say to Ralph Harenc, Breteuil?" Father finally spoke, his voice an angry rumble.

"I…I…Harenc spoke ill of me and stole from the castle treasury to feather his own nest in case I should replace him!"

"Prove it!" snapped Harenc. "What you claim is but the fevered workings of your greed-filled mind!"

"Ralph Harenc speaks truth," said the King. "Nothing has been stolen. I have examined the accounts personally."

Eustace's face turned even redder.

"You have committed an evil act, Eustace of Breteuil," continued Father, "not only against Ralph Harenc and his son but against me, your Duke, your King, and your father-by-marriage. You placed me in a terrible position. I could not favour you and waive punishment when you committed such a vile transgression against this man and his child. To do so, would make me seem partisan. I am the Lion of Justice. Justice must be served, no matter how painful it is for you—or for me."

My heart began to race, flopping heavily in my throat. Where were my daughters? Why was he talking so and not bringing them forward?

Stiffly Henry rose from his seat, making the candleflames swirl and flicker. He looked old, almost bent.

"The words are clear in the Holy Bible of our Lord God, written in Leviticus," he said. "If a man causes an injury to his neighbour; as he has done, so shall it be done to him; breach for breach, eye for eye…"

"No!" Eustace suddenly shouted, waving his arms in a mad panic. "You will not take my eyes!"

Father looked sad, painfully sad. "I do not want your bloody eyes, you revolting, grovelling dung-heap. When news of your calumny reached me, Ralph Harenc made a special request, as he was entitled to do as the injured party. I agreed with heavy heart and rode to Ivry at once."

Suddenly I knew…I *knew* what my Father was hinting at, what he had not said outright.

An eye for an eye….

"Sire, where are my children?" I screamed, panicking and losing control of myself.

The King gestured towards the curtain again. A nurse emerged holding on to two pitiful, small, familiar figures. They tripped, staggered, bashed into each other and the nurse's stout legs. They wept and wailed, afraid and in pain. Like little Roger Harenc, they wore bandages over their eyes but their wounds were fresh and wept through the layered cloth.

But there was worse. Not only had my beautiful daughters been blinded but their noses were cut at the tip, deforming their pretty features. As awful as it was for a mother to think, in those moments of horrified shock, I thought they resembled little pigs rather than children.

A dreadful wailing scream filled the chamber. The King walked away as did Ralph Harenc, who shouted, "Justice has been done. Roger is avenged."

The screeching went on. I suddenly realised the awful sound came from within me, an animal sound emitted from somewhere deep inside my soul, somewhere that boiled with grief and animalistic rage.

On the dais, my two wounded daughters clutched each other and sobbed, recognising my anguished voice but unable to see where I was.

Still wailing, I stepped in their direction, arms outstretched, but then all that had befallen that day overwhelmed my senses, and I collapsed in a swoon on the flagstones. Darkness rushed over me, heavy as a shroud.

CHAPTER TWELVE

The journey back to Breteuil was dreadful beyond words. I sat in a chariot with my mutilated children, trying to offer words and acts of comfort. They would not respond, would not allow me to touch them; they clung to each other as if fearing I would wound them further. Between spells of horrible muteness, they would turn to each other and weep, drawing their matted hair over their faces like veils to hide the mucus that ran, unimpeded, from their ruined nostrils.

I still blamed Eustace for his deed but my blazing anger towards him was dying to cold embers. The hatred in my heart was now directed towards Father. King he might be, a duty he might have, but I deemed he had broken the greatest rule of all—to protect his family. He should have never suggested Peronelle and Lora as hostages in the first place. He played a foolish game, tempted fate with their lives; Eustace, idiot that he was, played the game—and lost. Or rather, our poor children lost.

Again, I reached out to Peronelle, so small, so tragic. She uttered a small cry and shied away. I began to weep. What would I do with my daughters? The raw wounds would heal but what then? No more tutors, no more dancing, no more embroidery. They would become the stuff of legend around Breteuil—the freakish, hideous daughters of the idiot count locked within a tower.

When we arrived at the castle, I had the servants hustle the girls into the nursery. People clustered in the bailey, staring. I presumed some rumour of what had happened had reached their ears already.

Once the girls were settled under the care of the nursemaids and Eustace's personal physician, I sought out my husband. He was in the solar, hunched over, weeping like a woman.

"Why do you weep?" I said harshly. "It is our daughters who have suffered. Their tears will fall for all time."

"I cannot bear it! I am a doomed man for the evil I've wrought!" he wailed.

"You must help put this right as much as it can ever be put right!" My voice was like thunder.

"How can I do such a thing? Tell me!"

"The King. With these violent actions, he has stepped outside the bounds of acceptable behaviour. He must have known Harenc's character—and yours, you bastard! He could have offered coin to Ralph Harenc as restitution; could have offered lands, castles, a lordship...anything. No, instead he handed over our daughters as if they were lambs for the table. Eustace—I will have my revenge on him, I swear it."

His harsh, unmanly weeping ceased; he glanced at me, red-eyed, a bit of his usual craftiness creeping into his expression. Focussing on Father's sins would lift some of the guilt from his shoulders. "What do you plan, Juliane?"

"Go to your castle at Pacy. Raise a rebellion. Tell all men the Duke of Normandy is an unnatural tyrant, a murderer who slew one brother, an anointed King, and unlawfully imprisoned another—and who has harmed his own granddaughters on a cruel whim. Henry is not loved here; he is already struggling with rebellious nobles. Perhaps even Louis of France will join your cause."

"What of you? What part will you play, Juliane?"

"What part would a woman play?" I said scornfully. "You will be the sword in my hand, husband. In becoming so, you will atone for your crime against Harenc's boy; against our daughters."

Mumbling, he lowered his head...but he nodded. Despite his show of reticence, I knew the idea of a rebellion appealed to the base and bloody side of his nature. The cretin probably still had his eye on the accursed Castle of Ivry too.

"I will do it, Juliane, but I fear leaving you here alone with William. What if Henry should come for our son? Or even for you."

"It is you the King will go after. I am, after all, but a weak woman of little value," I said sarcastically. "William is a different matter, but if things become too fearsome here, I will send him away to a hidden refuge. Do not argue with me, Eustace. It is the only way we can ever know peace. We must bring my Father down."

Breathing heavy and laboured, he clambered unsteadily to his feet. "It will be done. As you say, many barons loathe Henry. I shall send to those who love not the English King, and head for my castle of Pacy where we shall converge and rise against him."

I nodded. "Good. But before you ready to departure, we must first decide—what shall become of Lora and Peronelle?"

He shrugged, helpless. "I…I do not know. The physician says their bodies will heal but…"

"Their minds never will," I finished. "It would be the natural wish of a mother's heart to keep them close, but common sense tells me this cannot be. They would live as captives in Breteuil; hearing life go on around them, yet unable to participate. They would need constant nursing, servants to help them mount the stairs, nurses to watch so that they would not fall from the heights or drown in the moat." I took a deep breath. "They must be sent away to safety, Eustace. To a convent. The holy sisters look after the injured and sick. When the girls are fully healed, they can then become nuns themselves. A life in prayer and contemplation in perpetual darkness is the best they can hope for—thanks to my Father's cruelty."

"Have you thought of which House might take them?"

I nodded again. "Fontevraud, near Chinon, the new foundation begun by Robert de Arbrissel. I have heard near to three thousand nuns dwell there, living under the rule of St Benedict. The abbess, Petronille de Chemille, is a decent and learned woman, by all accounts. I will write to her in regards to our daughters' futures."

"And if she will not accept two blinded girls as nuns?"

"She will, I am certain of it," I said. "I will send her a gift she cannot refuse." I made a motion with my hand as if rubbing coins betwixt finger and thumb. "Abbeys are always in need of money. Acquisitive, these men and woman of God! Still, I must not complain. Not if they agree to care for our children and give them a vocation—and a reason to live."

Eustace rode out for Pacy, taking many men with him but leaving a stout team of defenders at Breteuil in the event of trouble. I did not expect any, even when news reached Father's ears of Eustace's uprising. I imagined that the King would march toward Pacy as quickly as possible to engage my husband in battle—it was wicked of me to think such thoughts, but maybe with any luck, the two of them would kill each other and solve everyone's problems.

Hastily I wrote to Abbess Petronille at the House of Fontevraud, asking for succour for my injured and helpless children. It pained me to tell her how they had reached this unhappy pass but I hoped the sorrowful tale would rouse her Christian charity.

It must have worked, for she responded promptly in the affirmative, telling me that she would accept Peronelle and Lora as nuns of the order. They were perhaps a little younger than she would have liked but not unduly so, and though it troubled her slightly that they had professed no vocation, she was sure it would come in time after the shock of their wounding had worn off. Christ, after all, loved the little children.

I breathed a sigh of relief. The girls would be safe, looked after for all of their natural lives. As soon as possible, I would have a carriage prepared and send them hence to Fontevraud—with a handsome gift for the Abbess as a token of my gratitude. The girls would have to be told first, however…

I stirred uneasily at the thought. Only in the last few days had they deigned to speak to me, their voices little and mouse-like, revealing nothing. Yes, no, please, thank you, was all they would say as they huddled together, their heads swathed in the white linen bandages. There hardly seemed my own children anymore but changelings, secretive and shy.

Taking a deep breath, I steeled myself to face them and strode down the corridors towards the nursery. Halfway along, I came upon my son, William, his brow creased with concern.

"Is there going to be a war, mother?" he asked, clutching my sleeve. "I bid you tell me the truth!"

"There may be," I opted for honesty.

"Will Father kill my Grandsire the King?"

"No…Well, maybe…I do not know."

"I hate the King for what he did to my sisters!" blurted William.

"So do I, William." Tears misted my eyes. I truly did; I hated him with every fibre of my being.

"I would fight him myself!" I looked at my poor, thin little son, coughing fitfully, a boy of almost fourteen looking closer to eleven or twelve, and the awful realisation came—it was unlikely he would fight anyone, ever. Eventually he might hold lands and learn the ways of a good lord, but it was doubtful he would ever ride into battle. I hugged him to me, although I could tell he was embarrassed by my display of emotion.

When I broke away, I said, "Now I must go speak to your sisters. It is, I fear, impossible for them to stay here. The kind Abbess of Fontevraud has offered to take them."

"I will miss them." William hung his head.

I ruffled his hair. "I will, too.' But in my heart, I knew my daughters, as they were, had already gone.

When I entered the nursery, the girls were standing by the window, hands entwined, twinned in misery. Their furled heads swung in my direction; they seemed aware of my presence as if, lacking eyes, their other senses had grown keen.

"Peronelle? Lora?" I said softly. "Would you sit?"

They inched over to their bed, climbed clumsily upon it, feeling around with splayed fingers. The nursemaid curtseyed and vacated the chamber.

"Your father and I have decided…"

"To send us away." It was Lora who spoke. It made me jump as the girls had both been so silent since their wounding.

"Yes. To Fontevraud Abbey. It is for the best."

"We are ugly and unwanted now." It was a statement.

"No, you are not," I started to protest.

"We are." Lora's pale pink lips curved up in a cynical little smile, one too old for such a young girl. "No one would ever marry us."

"No one," echoed Peronelle, piping up. She fidgeted, playing with her heavy bandages.

"That is not why you must go." I sounded angrier than I had intended. "It is for your own safety."

"Safety," murmured Lora, that hard little smile still lingering.

I blushed to the roots of my hair, glad that the girls could not see my shame. I should have kept them safe; should have done more to protect my daughters. Once again, a stab of rage towards the King tore through me. A brute, who did what he wanted to get what he wanted. A lecher who lay with anything in skirts. A possible regicide. A blinder of children…

"Take us away, as you will" Lora's voice broke into my reverie. "Make us safe."

"Safe," repeated Peronelle. "Safe in the dark."

I sent the girls to Fontevraud early the next morning. From the walls, I watched their chariot wind down the hill toward the town, eyed by curious passers-by—peasants in rough homespun, a shepherd with an injured lamb slung over his broad shoulders, a goodwife holding two little maids by the hand. Perfect little children, glowing with life and good health. Children unlike mine.

Embittered, I turned away from the sight, my squirrel-fur cloak wrapped tightly around my shoulders against the bite of the wind.

And in the distance, approaching Breteuil from the west, I saw a slow-moving column of men, both on foot and on horseback, the dust from the hooves of the heavy warhorses rising in huge clouds. Over them soared the distinctive banner of the Duke of Normandy, the King of England.

Father had not gone to lay siege to Pacy or to meet in battle with Eustace and his rebels.

He was coming here to lay waste to Breteuil, no doubt to take me as a prisoner to use against my husband, to take my sickly son, maybe blind him as he had his sisters. I had made a mistake, a terrible mistake in presuming he would target Eustace instead of me…

"William!" I screamed, almost knocking the archer on the wall-embrasure to his doom as I rushed past to descend the stairs. As I half-ran, half-fell down the steps, I could hear bells tolling an alarm in both castle and town. Thanks to Almighty God, someone other than I had spotted the King's army.

I found William in the chapel, pale with fright as he listened to the stony, threatening bells; the chaplain was attempting to comfort him, speaking of God's Will and such-like. "Father Osmund," I said, "I beg you, take my son and go from the castle sally-port; I will see it stays open a while longer until swift horses are brought and you are safely away. Ride for a monastery, for any kind of sanctuary—anywhere; keep my boy safe, even if you must hide like an outlaw in the forest."

The priest's mouth opened and shut like that of a fish hauled from the water with no sound emerging but he managed to nod.

"William," I said to my son. "Go with the good Father Osmund. Ride at his side and do not look back. *Do not look back*!"

"What about you, Mother?" he said, eyes bright with fear. Eyes. Eyes that must stay as clear and shining blue as they were this bitter day.

"I shall be fine, William. I can deal with your grandfather, I promise you. Now go!"

Father Osmund and William scuttled from the chapel and ran down the hall, the priest's cassock flapping like a sail in the wind of his speed.

Breathing heavily, I leant against the chill chapel wall below a wooden icon of the Virgin embedded into the stonework. Would the walls of Breteuil hold against my Father? Perhaps I could beat him off until Eustace, whose spies would soon inform him of the King's intentions, could bring his own forces up behind him and crush his might with horsemen and spearmen, a hammer smashing Henry's forces against the anvil that was the stout masonry of Breteuil.

I forced myself into action, summoning my servants, my guards. I sent one man to ascertain that William and Father Osmund were gone from Breteuil, then gave orders that the town gates be closed and barred to both arrivals and leave-takers. Barrels of pitch were hauled to the top of the castle gatehouse and archers bristled on every tower, their numbers tripled.

I summoned the steward to the Great Hall; he rushed in, flushed, jittery, and clearly quite terrified. "Have you had news of the mood in the town?" I queried.

"Yes, milady." He glanced away.

"Look at me, man! What is wrong?"

"There is great fear amongst the townsfolk."

"That is to be expected; the King of England is without the walls and likely in no happy mood."

He swallowed; a prominent Adam's apple bobbed in his throat. "Many say they will not hold the gate against their Duke."

"Bastards!" I cried, hands curling into fists. This was what I had feared most. Betrayal. "Bastards…and cowards!"

"It is not a sure thing, Lady," said the steward. "They may find their mettle yet. And who knows, we have not heard from King Henry's heralds as yet; we do not know his purpose here."

"I am sure it is not a good one," I said, "but you are correct—it would not do well to act too hastily. We will wait until the King sends a herald."

Dressed in my best bliaut and a rose-red cloak, I sat on the dais in the Great Hall and waited. Mercifully, my wait was not for long. I heard the cries of the watch, the grinding of the portcullis as it was raised into upright position. A short while later one of Father's heralds was escorted into the chamber, a lean-legged man with a hawk's beak nose and a bowl of blue-black hair. The Lion on his tabard snarled out at me, a threat. He bowed, arrogance and annoyance flowing from his person.

"Speak, herald," I said from my high seat. "What do you have to say to me? Why does my sire the King approach with a war-like host?"

"The Lord King and Duke of Normandy, his Highness Henry First Of That Name sends a message to the Countess Juliane de Breteuil. He wonders why, in his own Dukedom of Normandy, the gates of one of his towns is barred against him. He wonders why his own loving daughter does not show the respect due him, as both Father and overlord, in accordance with the laws of Almighty God and the realm."

My lips tightened. "Herald, you may take a message back to my sire right away. Listen carefully, for I want him to hear it all—I bar my gates against him because we are now enemies and always shall be until the end of time. He may well, upon hearing this news, seek to batter his way in. However, such actions will bring him only infamy—minstrels will sing in mockery of how he makes war on women when Count Eustace, master of this house, is not in residence. As for being his loving daughter—love has turned to bitterest hate through his cruel, unnatural and tyrannical actions. Herald, you may tell his Grace the King these words—Juliane of Breteuil, from this day forth, has no father save He that dwells in Heaven, who is a kind and merciful Father, unlike her earthly one!"

The Herald's face had become a lump of ice. "You refuse to admit the King, my Lady?"

"I refuse. If he truly wants to see me, he must fight for the right."

"Then Countess—it is farewell!" The man gave a deep, sharp bow and retreated towards the doorway.

I listened to the sound of his boots on the flagstones as he hurried away. Now, all I could do was wait—and hope that Father would think a siege too troublesome and turn aside from Breteuil to deal with the true threat, Eustace's rebellion at Pacy.

Night had fallen. I was uneasy for there was no sign of Father's armies moving from their position outside the gate. When I stood on the walls of the castle to observe, I could see his men's campfires glowing in the night-fog and hear the rumbling ruckus of the camp.

Wrapped in a hood grey mantle that made her look a ghost, Cecelie joined me on the walls. The night's dampness clung to us both; above, the moon soared through a patch of flying cloud. It was cold, our breaths mist before our lips; it was Lenten time, the winter nearly done, but the weather still tending towards coldness. Below the castle's slopes, the lake glimmered, a full silver mirror reflecting broken images of the moon. Closer to us, at the foot of the battlements, the waters of the moat juddered as the rising wind disturbed their stillness. Flecked with patchy ice around the edges, the murky depths were full of old leaves and churned up mud, products of the recent thaw.

"Milady Juliane, it is too cold to stay up here," said Cecelie, proffering a second cloak to me, which I took with gratitude. I wrapped my hands in its heavy folds; my fingers were so cold, they were blue, the colour of a dead man's. "It will do no one any good, you catching your death out in this wind. I expect the King will merely wait out the night at Breteuil and then march away at first light."

"You are likely right," I said, merely to appease her, for I was not so certain. "Still, I cannot sleep knowing he is without the walls." I stared along the wall-walk at the archers leaning in embrasures, tense shouldered, the goose-feather fletchings of their arrows a-flutter. Fire braziers burned at intervals, casting out meagre light and even less heat. The wind at that height was a constant scourge, the last breath of winter biting the castle's defenders with icy teeth.

"At least come in for a while," coaxed Cecelie. "I will warm some wine for you; put rich spices in it."

I decided to relent; my nose dripped, my eyes were sore and weeping from the chill gale. Allowing her to take my arm, we began to walk toward the stairs—but suddenly thunderous noise filled the air, a resounding crash that echoed through the town's streets and up to the castle.

"Jesu!" I tore free of Cecelie's grasp and ran to the wall, where I leaned dangerously far out over the machicolations, seeking to see what had happened.

In the town, warning bells began to boom and jangle again, fearful, discordant. Fires leapt up by the eastern gate. I saw a few arrows fly, limned against the fires—but if that was meant as a defence from the town, it was a half-hearted one. Another boom sounded, louder than the first. Now faint screams and shouts drifted to my ears, even above the tolling of the bells.

"What—what is happening, mistress?" stammered Cecelie, close to my ear. She sounded near to tears.

"A ram...they must be using a ram. My father is trying to break his way into the town. He is going to make war on his own daughter. Maybe I should not be surprised, for this is a man who even wreaks his wrath on innocent children!"

I ran from the wall, down the stairs and into the Great Hall, with Cecelie in hot pursuit. Just at that moment a messenger burst in, puffing and gasping, his tabard half torn from his body, his face stained with sweat and smoke. "My Lady, "he shouted. "be prepared for attack. The Duke of Normandy has led his forces into Breteuil! The gate is down!"

"Who are you, that brings this news?"

"Eudo le Grande, a guard from the Eastgate. The King's battering ram was mighty, with a head of iron—it smashed the timbers to pieces."

"And you left your post?" Anger and panic reared crazily within my breast.

"It was that…or die, Countess. His Grace is not in a merciful mood. Besides, the town has surrendered; the mayor strode out, bold as brass, with a white flag and laid it before the hoofs of Henry's warhorse. All the people cheered the Duke's arrival and he has promised that if they loyally support his cause, he will not fire the town, nor will he allow looting or the ravishment of women."

"All traitors, all craven traitors!" I cried. "All these years and the townsfolk still care nothing for their lord and lady, who have done so much for their welfare!"

Leaving the soldier, I raced out of the keep and toward the castle gates. The garrison was in place; more braziers burned, and men were balanced over the murder-holes in the barbican, some armed with rocks, others stoking the flames behind a huge iron pot filled to the brim with pitch.

One of the captains, a soldier I knew by the name of Herve de Mer, rushed in my direction. "My Lady Countess, you must go back to the safety of the keep. It is too dangerous for you here."

"I must face this danger; it is my duty!" I cried, and pushing my way through the stunned men in the guardhouse, climbed into one of the projecting towers facing out over the town. Thrusting a surprised archer aside, I pressed my face to a narrow arrow-slit. Ahead, beyond the tall spires of the Abbey of Our Lady of Breteuil, built by an ancient count called Gilduin and surrounded by monks' fishponds and vineyards, past the numerous parish churches and the crooked merchants' houses of timber and stone, past Baker's Row with its roaring ovens and the long, winding Street of Silversmiths, I could see men marching, filling the streets from side to side, looking at this distance like an anthill kicked over to expel a host of angry ants.

As they drew closer, Father became visible, riding in the forefront with his captains around him. He was mounted on a heavy-set stallion with an ugly head and mean eyes; its body was armoured, a spike jutted from its petrel, making it resemble a demonic unicorn.

Father wore his helm, a sharp cone with a nose-guard flaring like a tusk, and his sword was visible at his side, the gem on its pommel winking in the gloom.

He led his troops up to the base of the hill where the castle stood, then raised his hand to signal a halt. Abruptly, the ranks parted, as along the road trundled a great siege engine on wheels, a trebuchet to hurl rocks at the castle walls to cause a breach. Such a machine could also be used to hurl flaming debris and set the wooden-roofed buildings in the outer ward aflame.

Breath erratic in my lungs, I stood in the freezing shadows, watching the lumbering engine approach the hill. I truly had not thought it would come to this. Now I knew that the King would slight Breteuil and imprison me to spite my husband before he went on to quell Eustace's rebellion.

Once again, cold rage burnt within my heart. How I loathed my father! I thought of Lora and Peronelle, their beauty marred, their vision stolen, their future one of darkness and dust, bound forever to the cloister. He had not only destroyed their lives but now he endeavoured to destroy my home. I wished I had a man's strength and knowledge of arms, the ability to call my sire to fight in a battle to the death, one on one…

Glancing down, I spotted Father's Herald, the hawk-nosed one, riding up the hill for a second time. I motioned to the gate guards and shouted, "No admittance to that rider…but I will speak to him."

As the man sat on his skittish horse below the frowning towers of the barbican, I leaned over the battlements of the projecting tower where I watched Father's progress toward me and called out, "What have you to say this time, Herald? What word from the tyrant, Henry of England?"

The Herald glanced up, squinting through the shadows. He looked nervous; doubtless aware that dozens of archers had their arrows trained on him, and that the burning pitch was not so far away. It was considered very bad form to kill a herald…but I would do it if I deemed it necessary. I had learnt ruthlessness from the best—my own father.

"His Grace the Duke of Normandy wishes his daughter Countess Juliane to know that if she surrenders the Castle of Breteuil within one day, all within its walls shall be spared punishment."

"And if I do not?" I yelled down. "I have a great supply-store and a deep well. I can hold out until Count Eustace comes to lift the siege. Which he will."

"Have you anything more to say, Countess?"

"No. Nothing."

"I will tell the Duke of Normandy your answer!" The Herald grasped his reins and set spurs to the flanks of his steed, making it leap forward unexpectedly and stumble down the icy hillside.

, Moving stiffly in his mail coat, Herve de Mer approached me. "My Lady, I insist that you seek out the safety of the keep. Soon, I fear, hostilities will begin."

I desired to stay in the gatehouse, watching events unfold, but I realised my presence would distract the soldiers, so I nodded sullen agreement and hurried toward the bulk of the great Tower. I had no sooner reached the second floor when I heard shouting and roaring from the bailey, followed by a whistling sound and a heavy thud.

Scurrying for the nearest window, I ripped open the wooden shutters. A huge chunk of stone lay teetering not ten feet from the keep's walls, having made a crater in the damp soil of the bailey.

The siege had begun.

All night long and through most of the day I listened to the thud, thud, thud of stones hitting the castle walls. Occasionally there was a crash as a boulder smote off a row of crenellations or took out the roof on a tower. Other rocks tumbled into the inner wards, shattering the smith's hut and killing two horses in the stables.

My archers continued to pelt the King's forces with arrows, picking off quite a few men who dared come to close; however, the men manning the trebuchet were well out of range. Again and again, the gigantic arm swung through the air; now the boulders had disappeared and the attackers were hurling horse-dung and dead animals. The whole bailey reeked of ordure, rotten flesh, pitch, sweat—and fear.

I was confident we had enough supplies to hold out for months, but I also was aware of Father's mercurial temper, his endless impatience. *He* would not wait for months, especially when he had insurrection throughout Normandy to quell. The thought of what he might do next set my uneasy mind a-whirl—perhaps he would roll the huge siege-tower *Malvoisin*, the Evil Neighbour, up to the castle walls, filling it with armoured warriors eager for bloodshed. But…Breteuil Castle was on a hill, making it difficult for such a Siege Tower to ascend, and with the drawbridge raised it would be almost impossible to cross the moat, especially since it was swollen by ice-melt and rain.

He could try to send assassins under the cover of darkness, fording the moat and seeking entrance at the postern gate or by climbing the privy chutes—but that, I surmised, would be a last-ditch attempt, for once inside his men would be in as much danger as the household and sorely outnumbered. He might also seek to find the source of our well-water and poison it, which was more worrisome, but I had tuns of ale which would last a long while yet if the water went bad.

Another lump thudded heavily into the courtyard, this time with a noisome splat. A dead horse—and it had been dead some time by the stench of it. Eyes and nose streaming, I pressed a kerchief to my face.

Suddenly there was a commotion amidst the archers massed on the turrets over the gatehouse. "Herald coming!" I heard one man cry, and the shout was taken up.

I began to run, hauling my skirts to almost indecent levels to gain the wall swiftly. As before, I peered out the tiny arrow-slit in the gate-tower to observe my foes clustered at the foot of the hill. Father was there, down at the bottom, mounted on his warhorse beneath his Lion banner; next to him, the arm of the trebuchet was still.

The Herald was approaching, coaxing his mount up the slippery flank of the hill. As he neared the moat, I called out to him in a great voice, "No further, Herald, lest my archers loose. The Lady of Breteuil is here. Deliver your message."

The Herald's head with its dinted conical helmet swung in my direction, although, hidden deep inside the Tower, he could not see me. "His Grace the Duke of Normandy sends another message to the Countess Juliane. If the gates are opened by sun-up, no one within the walls of the fortress will be harmed; all shall receive pardons. However, if the siege is extended and men and supplies from the royal army wasted on taking Breteuil, severe penalties shall be paid. For every day that is spent outside the castle gates, a man, woman or child will go to the gallows."

Blood pounded in my temples. This violent reaction from Henry was what I had feared. I knew, too, it was no idle threat meant only to terrify. Almost as if of their own volition, my hands fluttered up to my face, touching the orbits of my eyes, tracing the fine bones there. Would my own father put my eyes out as he had done to my daughters?

I thought of the castle household; innocent folk dragged into this conflict. *My* responsibility. While some of them probably would die for my cause, I refused to ask them to do so.

My daughters were safe in Fontevraud. My son William was, pray God, with the chaplain behind the stout walls of an abbey with the right of Sanctuary.

I was going to have to surrender and take whatever punishment Father saw fit to give. Imagining the horror of mutilation, I touched my face again. A sudden harsh, fierce flame kindled in my breast. I might surrender the gate but no, I would not give in. Lora and Peronelle would be avenged. *I* would be avenged—even if it cost me my life.

I turned to one of the soldiers stationed in the gatehouse, a short bluff fellow wearing old-fashioned boiled leather studded with rusty metal rings. He was carrying a crossbow, a cruel weapon and a deadly one. Men sometimes recovered if struck by an ordinary arrow; not so a crossbow bolt, which crushed bone with great force. The crossbow's reputation was such that Pope Urban, speaking at the Lateran Synod, had (ineffectively) banned them for use against Christian men. Inhuman, he had called them. The Devil's Work.

Devil's work…Well, Father had acted the devil with my daughters and his acts were hardly full of Christian mercy.

"You there!" I said to the crossbowman. "Give me your weapon!"

"My lady?" Captain de Mer, who was also in the guardroom, glanced nervously in my direction. "You are not going to shoot the Herald, are you?"

"Of course not—that would be a wicked act contrary to the rules of warfare," I said. "I have another purpose for it. Here man, do not delay."

With some reluctance, the old soldier handed me the crossbow. It was heavy and I had never shot a bolt before but I had watched the men practice many a time. I could do it. *I had to do it.*

Breathing deeply, I shouted out to the Herald, who still lingered on the hill, awaiting answer. "Go back to Henry, Duke of Normandy and King of England. Tell him that at dawn tomorrow, Juliane de Breteuil shall open the gates to allow his free passage. The castle will surrender to his Grace."

The sun rose in a glorious crimson welter the next morning. I watched from the wall as the drawbridge was lowered and the great gates of carved oak, their surfaces striped with sheets of beaten metal, slowly opened. Down below, my Father gave a signal to his followers and began making his way up the hill with his troops surging behind him.

I called Cecelie and Idonea to me in the solar, kissed both of them upon the cheek. "You have been good maids to me all these years. Now, go and attend to your own families; you have done all you can for mine."

"Lady, I worry for you," said Idonea uneasily. "I do not want to leave you."

"You must—it is my last order to you."

"Last..." Cecelie gasped, pressing her hand to her mouth in shock.

"Just a figure of speech," I lied. "Now go!"

Clutching each other for support, tears streaming from their eyes, my two ladies-in-waiting fled, vanishing into corridors inside the castle.

I sat down on a stool, surrounded by padded cushions, the crossbow hidden beneath my flowing crimson skirts. I sent a page to take a message to the chamberlain: "Tell him to inform the King I am in the solar. I will receive him there, and there I will officially hand the castle over to his keeping."

The boy ran out of the room; I listened to his footsteps pattering away into the distance. I sipped some wine, willing my nerves to calm. Hysteria would avail me not. My hand must be steady.

I was going to kill the King of England. *My Father...my enemy...*

After what seemed an eternity, I heard the tramp of heavy feet in the corridor beyond the solar. It was him—I recognised his firm tread.

A moment later, Henry's shadow darkened the arch of the doorway. He stepped in, mail jingling, his helmet gone but his coif still on. He looked irritable, whey-faced and old. The hate writhing in my heart was so strong at the sight of him that bile rose into my mouth.

"Ah, Juliane, you've led me a merry dance," he muttered. "How could you have behaved in such a foolish manner? I thought you were cleverer than that."

I bowed my head. "I was distraught, Father; you know why."

"Yes, yes, I know, a nasty business, but you understand why it happened, do you not? I had to remain impartial, I could not favour Eustace when he was, beyond all doubt, the aggressor."

*A nasty business...*I gazed at him with eyes grown ice-cold. "Business, that was all they were to you. Your own granddaughters, who trusted you."

A flush of anger purpled his visage. "We will talk of this matter no more! It is done! I have had enough of your waywardness. Pah, I need a drink!"

Turning his back to me, he stomped over to the table where I had left a wine decanter and two goblets.

My chance was here!

Bending over, I tore the hidden crossbow from beneath my skirts, my sweaty fingers grappling to get the bolt in the groove and draw back the string.

"I was always good to you, Juliane," the King was grumbling as poured the wine. A jet of red hit the cup like a fountain of blood. "It is a pity of course for the girls, but life is harsh; a lesson you must learn…"

And you too, Father…

I released the trigger. The crossbow kicked back against me, making me stagger and nearly lose my footing. The bolt shot across the chamber towards the King—and missed. It thunked into the wall and fell clattering to the floor.

"Christ's Teeth!" roared Father, whirling on his heel, as swift as a striking snake. The goblet he was lifting went over; wine sprayed across the room. I tried to run but was caught in my own skirts.

Father was upon me in an instant, throwing me to the ground and kneeling over me, dragging my arms behind my back. I tried to bite him but he moved too fast and was far too strong.

"You murderous little bitch!" he gasped, his tone full of both rage and amazement. "I did not see *that* coming!"

"Satan himself has spared his own!" I cried and spat at his face in rage.

Spittle running down his cheek, the King roared for his men. Soldiers descended on the solar, milling around, their muddied boots leaving tracks across the floor. My hands were bound by a sturdy rope and I was hauled unceremoniously to my feet.

"See that the drawbridge is destroyed!" Father thundered to one of his captains. "Let no one come in or out of the castle. Put the garrison and all the household under arrest! Seize and impound all items of value."

"The household has done nothing except serve me!" I screamed, fighting my bonds. "Leave my servants be, I beg you!"

"Be silent!" ordered Father, eyes blazing. "This is my castle now and I shall do as I please."

"Your Grace, shall we take the Countess to the dungeons?" asked one gap-toothed, squab-nosed thug in a stained blue tabard. He leered at me as if he wished nothing more than to get me in a corner of a dark cell.

"No, leave her with me."

"But…what she has done is treason!" said the knight, perplexed,

"Do not question me, oaf—I am your bloody King!" Father raised his fist as if to strike the fool. "Now, all of you, do as I have bidden! Get the fuck out!"

As swiftly as they had arrived, the soldiers hastened away. I was left with Father. "Come with me, you snapping she-wolf!" he snarled, dragging me across the floor by the rope that scored my wrists. "I have special plans for you!"

He hauled me down the corridor and then forced me on hands and knees to climb up one of the staircases leading to the wall. Whipped by the wind, we stood together on the height, mere inches apart. I thought he was minded to kill me for my treachery, maybe stab me to the heart in front of all those watching from the bailey below as a warning to others.

"For all that you have done," he spat, "you are still my daughter. I will not execute you, for your actions, I deem, were not done with true malice but with the unpredictable emotions of a woman. I am going to give you a chance to go free, Juliane…"

Perplexed, I stared at him. How could I go free? He'd confiscated everything in the castle and even now I heard the sound of axes chopping at the wooden struts of the drawbridge.

"You want to go? You want your life? Well, then, jump, Juliane. Jump into the moat and swim for safety. For freedom."

I stared down. The grey waters loomed, undulating, filled with floating chips of ice. I might survive, I might not, depending on how hard I hit the surface. Depending on if my heavy gown dragged me under to a frigid death…

"I'll sink in these clothes," I murmured.

"Well, take them off then!" sneered Father with a nasty grin. "Go on. You are clearly shameless. Do it, before I lose my patience and decide you should hang!"

With clumsy fingers I tore at my garments, stripping down to my thin chemise. Near enough naked, I stood shivering on the wall as the wind buffeted me. A crowd had gathered in the bailey and on the nearby towers, watching me; Father's men with evil leers and lascivious glances.

"Go!" snapped the King.

I jumped, my hair flowing out like a black cloud, my chemise, filled with wind from my sudden downward plunge, riding up around my waist, leaving my entire lower half bare to the elements and the eyes of my enemies. I heard shouts of laughter and a volley of obscene remarks seconds before my bare buttocks struck the surface of the water with painful force.

I went under, sinking like a stone. Desperately I flailed in the murk, fighting leaves and weeds and the pervasive, bone-chilling cold to reach the surface. Gasping, my head broke through the waters and I struck out swimming towards the land.

Crawling onto the muddy bank, I staggered to my feet, bruised, battered and humiliated. My sodden, stained chemise clung to the contours of my body, further adding to my shame. I began to run, or rather, hobble away. Laughter followed me.

I dared not look back.

CHAPTER THIRTEEN

There were a few loyal folk left in Breteuil. As I climbed from the moat and stumbled into a clump of nearby trees, wracked by violent shivers and my teeth chattering so hard I thought they'd break, I was approached by a burly, bearded man who had evidently hidden in the foliage watching my dive from the castle wall. I jumped back in terror at first, fearing he might assault me but he raised his open hands palm-up in a gesture of peace. "Milady, please, I beg you, do not fear me. I am here to help."

Before I could even answer, he swept off his huge woollen cloak and draped it around my shoulders. I clutched it to me, savouring the warmth, uncaring that it was rank with dog-hairs and the hem was stained with sheep-shite. "T—thank you…" I stammered, still unable to control my shaking. "W—who are you? I…I will see the Count rewards you."

"I am Thomas the Shepherd who lives upon the ridge beyond the town." He waved his arm in a vague westerly direction. "Milady, you probably won't remember, but when one year we lost most of the flock to a murrain and could not pay our rents, you interceded on our behalf with the Count and he waived the money. The wife and I are eternally grateful; we'd have starved otherwise."

I nodded weakly. I did not remember him but recalled the murrain, which killed whole herds of cattle and sheep.

"Come with me, milady. Quickly!" The shepherd gestured away into the trees. "It is not safe here with the King's soldiers on the prowl. I'll take you to my cottage; my wife can find you some clothes and tend any injuries."

I only half-trusted him—I trusted no man any more, for all seemed faithless—but what choice did I have? I could not travel in wet garments in February; I would have escaped Breteuil Castle only to die of the cold. Wrapped in the man's winter cloak, I limped along after him as he trudged through the woodlands. Every now and then, he halted and glanced at me to make sure I was still on my feet, but he seemed too afraid to touch me as I clambered over roots and mossy rocks.

At length, the trees parted and the ground sloped upwards. To my relief, a cottage stood on the top of the rise, surrounded by pens full of bleating sheep. The door opened and a stout woman in a white coif, grimy apron and wooden clogs stepped over the threshold.

"Who's this, Thomas? Oh my!" she shrieked as she saw me.

Then she was running through the mud, bundling me in her brawny arms and pulling me into the one-room cottage with its smoky fire and dried herbs rattling in bags along the worm-eaten rafters.

Over the next few days, the goodwife Jeannot made me some clothes out of an old blue dress she had stored in a wooden box. "It were my wedding dress, Lady," she said, as I tried it on and she adjusted it where necessary; it was a great shapeless thing but woollen and warm. "Alas, though, I have three great huge lumps of boys and no daughters. You're so lucky you have two pretty girls…"

Tears began to fall at that, my emotions fragile after all the dreadful events that had befallen, and I spilt out the truth of why the King and I were at odds, and why I had ended up swimming in the moat. Jeannot, less reserved than her husband Thomas, hugged me and cosseted me like babe as I wept and wailed on the dirt floor of the hut, the homestead dogs sniffing around me and mice scuttling through the thatching above my head.

"Oh, milady, neither me nor Thomas had any idea. We'd heard rumours the little girls were sent away but we thought it were for their education. I can see why you loathe his Grace…My God, if my father—God rot him, he was a temperamental old drunk—had dared injured any of my bairns…" She made a threatening fist with her hand. "I'd have gone for 'im too."

I wiped my tears, sniffed, and pulled my unruly black hair into a knot at the nape of my neck. "You are a good woman, Jeannot, and I won't forget what you and Thomas have done for me. But now I need to go to my husband at Pacy."

"Of course you must go; you're a great lady and will be needing to get back to the comforts of a castle. But it's a long road to Pacy—how do you plan to get there with no money and no entourage?"

"I don't know…" I said feebly.

"I thought that might be a problem," said Jeannot, beaming. "So I was talking with Thomas last night while you slept. He was left an old nag by an uncle who died without family and we haven't a clue what to do with the beast—we're sheep people, we are—and the horse just eats up hay and causes a nuisance. You can have the nag, Lady, to do with as you will. As for an entourage, I know it's only one man, but my eldest, Maurice, has said he'd see you safely to Pacy; I know you've not met him but he's a strong lad, built like an ox, and knows how to use cudgel and dagger against thieves and the like. "

"You are too kind," I said, "but it will take your Maurice so far from home, and then he will have to return on his own."

"We're free peasants," said Jeannot, "not serfs, milady. It's what he's always wanted, truth be told—to see the world beyond Breteuil, maybe find work somewhere else."

I could see no other way to reach Eustace. So, mounted on Thomas and Jeannot's inherited, sway-backed mare, grey as a mountain and lumpy as one too, I set out for Pacy, the bridle held by a massive-shouldered peasant in a leather hood, who grinned like a loon with the honour of his new position as guard and guide.

A King's daughter. Now I looked the Queen of Fools instead!

Reaching Pacy, there was some confusion at the castle gatehouse when I turned up with my large, cudgel-wielding companion. "Admittance?" shrilled the swivel-eyed sentry. "A country dullard accompanied by a trull? Not a chance, unless you can prove you've got business with the Count."

Maurice swung his cudgel menacingly; with his shock of red hair and gapped teeth, he resembled nothing less than a troll, a lumpen monster believed in by the forebears of the Norman race. "You should have respect for the Lady!"

"Why should I?" said the rat-faced little man, who I noted had a wineskin concealed under his cloak. "Lots of trollops come in here, they're all the same…"

I pushed back the hood of my warm, borrowed cloak, revealing my face. "Well, you had best learn some respect for *this* 'trollop'."

Visage blanching, the man stared at me with mouth agape. The wineskin fell from his hand and emptied all over the cobblestones. "My Lady Countess!" he gibbered.

"The same. Now open this bloody gate before I have you flogged."

My meeting with Eustace was a strange one. We met in the Great Hall without a single embrace or word of affection. For me, at any rate, there was no affection left. I was at Pacy purely from a sense of duty—and because there was no other place to go. Eustace was staring at me as if he thought I might draw a hidden crossbow and murder him on the spot. A few feet away, Maurice, rewarded for his pains with a hefty bag of coin, munched greedily on a cooked chicken brought fresh from the castle kitchens. Juices trickled in rivulets down his bristly chin as he held the carcass in both hands and took greedy bits from it.

"Stop eyeing me in that way, husband. I am not going to harm you," I said at last, with exasperation.

Eustace ran his hand through his hair; newly-cropped for war, it stuck up in strange red whorls. "Why did you do it?"

"You know why!"

"I wish you had not come here, Juliane! Once he finds out, he will hunt you. We'll both die."

My lips twisted into a mocking smile. "You already a traitor, remember? Your life is forfeit unless you can galvanise your rebels into swift action against the King. What *is* happening with the rebellion?"

He glowered, folding his arms over his chest. "The rebellion is over."

I had guessed no definite action had been taken but his reply startled me. "Over?"

"Half the barons were full of talk, no more," he said angrily. "They drifted away like morning mist. Not one castle was taken, not one battle fought. And now Henry will come to Pacy and have us both beheaded—or worse. Perhaps we could flee to France or beyond—Italy maybe."

"I will not run," I said wearily. "If the block is my fate, so be it. Go, if it is your wish."

He stayed. I wondered if he still cared for me in some small manner, although I guessed it probably was more a case of pride; he would not flee while a woman waited alone to face an angry monarch.

We retired to wait, together yet separate. We spoke civilly enough; he inquired about William, relieved to find that he was secreted away in a monastery alongside our chaplain. The truth hung heavy between us, though; because of our actions, it was unlikely our son would have any inheritance at all. Maybe he would stay in the monastery; he had always inclined towards books rather than warfare due to his frailty.

When we finally saw banners approach the gates of Pacy Castle, however, it was not the King leading an army to capture and destroy us. It was my brother Richard surrounded by a small retinue.

After he had greeted Eustace with all solemnity, the two men regarding each other with suspicion since they were now on the opposite sides of conflict, Richard asked permission to speak to me in private. Eustace readily agreed.

I took my brother to the small solar, dark with smoke, the walls chequered by faded chevrons and lozenges in green and red paint. I reclined on a stool; he sat opposite me, face grim. "Why did you do it, Juliane?" he asked.

"Why does everyone ask me that?" I said crossly. "First Eustace, now you. You would understand if it were your children who were maimed!"

"You know why Father blinded them. Blame Eustace for his actions…"

"I do blame him. He and Father were both to blame. Lora and Peronelle should never have been designated as hostages. But why bring up the rights and wrongs of it now? What's done is done, and I tried to murder the King of England, and most likely shall die on the block for such treason. I don't think Father truly expected I would survive my leap from Breteuil Castle; he'll pursue me to a bloody end. Eustace will die too, as a rebel, and my son will have no inheritance, no future. I accept my sins and my punishment."

Richard shook his head. "Juliane, Father is not going to kill you, or Eustace."

Dubiously I glanced at my brother. "What? How do you know? Clemency would be wondrous in a man who allowed his own granddaughters to be blinded with his blessing."

"I will not lie—he was in a rage after you survived your stunt at Breteuil and wanted to hunt you down like a dog. At first. However, you know his temper, it flows like the sea, sometimes swelling high, sometimes sinking low. The fire went out of him and instead of raging, he sank into misery over what had occurred. I knelt before him and spoke up for you, Juliane; I interceded with the King on your behalf."

"Oh, Richard." A lump came into my throat and I clasped his hand in my own. "I could not have had a better brother."

"Father said he will pardon both you and Eustace," Richard continued, "but only on one condition…"

"What is that?"

"You must seek him out in person and kneel at his feet, begging for forgiveness."

The thought of entering my sire's presence again was nauseating, but I knew I had to do it. Otherwise, I would remain a hunted woman and my son a pauper. Eustace might not like the idea of kneeling at Henry's feet—but I would force him to see sense.

"I will do it," I said to Richard. "Take the message to the King. The Countess and Count of Breteuil shall come to beg his forgiveness."

Father kept us on our knees for an eternity. Heads bowed, we crouched at his feet on the frigid tiles, mere inches from his gold-striped shoes. Outside we heard the Angelus Bell boom—a call to prayer and a time to spread good will.

There did not seem to be much good will in the King's chamber.

The light in the window-slits faded to black; servants scurried around, robes rustling faintly as they lit hundreds of tapers. My hands were numb, my knees frozen, my head pounding. Yet I dared not move for fear of giving offence.

At last, the King made a coughing noise. "You may both rise."

Stiffly, we got to our feet.

"Like Jesu, the Light of Our World," said Henry, his tone tinged with sarcasm, "I am full of forgiveness. You are both pardoned and free to go."

"Your Grace…" Eustace hurled himself back to the ground, grasping Father's hand and kissing his ring with fervour. "Your kindness and mercy will never be forgotten."

Father snatched his hand away; his eyes were narrowed. "Do not mistake my good nature for stupidity, though," he said. "You go with your lives, but I am stripping you of all castles save that of Pacy, where you shall live under my eye. And if I ever hear tell of any plots against your rightful liege-lord, you will both find yourselves in the dungeons…or dead. Now go."

We left Father's castle and rode through the night without stopping, sombre and silent, glad our ordeal was over.

At Pacy I put my mind to making a little garden full of bushes that butterflies loved to visit. Peronelle had been particularly fond of butterflies before her mutilation—she had chased them through the flowerbeds but never dared trap them in the prison of her hands. I wondered if, in her dark world, she still remembered their jewel-like wings whirring in the sunlight…

Despite my attempt to regain some of my old life, I still harboured hatred of Father deep within my soul. Every night I prayed God would see fit to punish him for all his evils.

And at last, on the twenty-fifth day of November, in the year of Our Lord Eleven-Hundred and Twenty, God took his revenge on Henry of England in a terrible and spectacular way.

Father was in Barfleur, ready to return to Winchester for the Christmas season. Thomas FitzStephen, a renowned sea-captain, offered him the use of his vessel, the White Ship, to make the crossing of the Narrow Sea. The King had already arranged his own transportation, so other members of the household took up FitzStephen's kind offer, among them William Adelin, my half-sister Matilda Countess of Perche, and my brother Richard.

Merry was the mood as the ship waited in the dock, and when the crew cried out for wine to cheer them before they fared across the freezing waves, William Adelin had it brought in great leather flagons and distributed it to all. Soon all sailors and passengers were extremely drunk, singing and dancing on the deck with abandon, throwing their empty goblets into the sea.

Ahead of them, the King's ship had slipped its moorings and was already gliding out of the harbour into the moonless night. Tipsy with drink, William Adelin shouted out, "FitzStephen, let us depart at once! I swear we can overtake the King's ship and reach England first! A fine race it would be!"

FitzStephen would not deny my half-brother, his prince; he, too, believed a race would prove good sport and an opportunity to show off the fleetness of his newly-refitted vessel. Swiftly the White Ship pulled away from the dock and sailed into the darkness— where it struck a hidden rock known as the Quillebœuf. Stern stone rent the hull asunder and the White Ship capsized, hurling many of the revellers into the frigid waters, trapping others inside its belly or below its broken timbers.

William Adelin, my father's only legitimate son, drowned trying to rescue poor Tilda, who was thrashing in the sea and calling out for help. My dear brother Richard, who had risked all to ask the King to spare his erring sister, also perished, sucked to his doom in the dark depths of the waters.

The King was beside himself, his wife dead, his heir swallowed by the raging tides. It was a just punishment by God—yet I was judged too and could feel no joy in his pain. I wanted to but I could not. William was my half-brother, and I had loved both Tilda and Richard dearly. I could not help but feel that alongside Father, the Almighty had punished me for my presumption, for failing to honour my sire, for trying to murder him at Breteuil.

Great darkness fell on me, body and soul. I was already estranged from Eustace but I could find no joy even in my son, William, who had, under King's orders, finally started learning of knighthood in another noble household—and thrived beyond our expectations.

I began to find solace in prayer and solitude and often visited the local convents to speak with the nuns. I thought of my sweet daughters in Fontevraud and began to long for them. I had not seen them or written to the Abbess since the day I sent them there. I had thought it kinder not to taunt them with news of a world they would never know—but now I knew not whom I had tried to protect. My daughters…or me?

News about my family reached me at Pacy every now and then. My half-sister Adelaide—Empress Matilda—was widowed and promptly remarried to Geoffrey of Anjou, an alliance forged to curb the growing threat of certain lords such as Amaury de Montfort, who had a brief reconciliation with Father and was granted Ivry, most likely to spite Eustace. Matilda loathed her new husband because, although known as 'Le Bel' for his beauty, Geoffrey was years younger than she and a hot-headed young man. Father had then gathered the barons in Winchester and Northampton and made them swear to crown Matilda Queen of England if he had no male heir. He had taken a second wife, Adeliza of Louvain, but despite his legendary fruitfulness, the marriage had produced no issue. Another judgment from God, perhaps.

In late November in the year of Our Lord Eleven-Hundred and Thirty-Five, Father over-indulged on a meal of lampreys, slimy eels which he loved to eat slathered with soured cream, and fell ill with gripings of the gut which the physician could not quell with any potion. His condition worsened, and on the first day of December, he passed into God's Keeping in the presence of Archbishop Hugh of Amiens, who had heard his last confession. His body was carried to Rouen, where he was embalmed and his entrails removed and sent to the priory of Notre Dame Du Pre. Then his flesh was salted to preserve it and his remains sewn into a bull's hide for the long journey to England.

Storms kept him from his final resting place at Reading Abbey for a month, but when he was at last buried near the high altar, it was not under the gaze of his daughter, Matilda, the rightful Queen of England, but Stephen of Blois, son of Father's sister Adela, who had usurped the throne from his cousin.

Again, it seemed, God had passed judgment on Father, even after death.

The next year Eustace died, suddenly and unexpectedly after cutting his hand on a dagger while on a hunt. I had no mind to marry again; indeed, I had lost the desire to live in the world of men with its squabbles over power and lands.

Peace called me, the quietude of the cloister. I decided to join Lora and Peronelle in the Abbey of Fontevraud. I would make amends to God there—and, if I could, to my maimed, blind daughters.

And so I am here in the nunnery cloisters, amid the cresset lamps, the cloying incense, the sweet tallowy smoke from the candles set in stone embrasures. The sound of the nuns singing in the choir floats up to God above and soothes the ears and mind of some…but never a sinner like me.

I pause. The veiled blind nuns, my daughters, have paused in front of the Chapter House door and are coming back, swiftly, purposefully.

Tap, tap, tap go their canes on the flagstones.

Will they speak, will they ask questions of me, their mother? Questions I cannot bear to answer? Will they speak at last to me of forgiveness?

Tap. Tap. Tap.

Lora in her sombre robes brushes by me without a single word, resentment flowing out from her like a dark, unhappy mist, her bitterness toward the mother who failed her yet undimmed by passing years, even though beneath her wimple I know the shorn golden curls are now flecked with grey.

Time does *not* heal all wounds, all griefs.

But Peronelle, my baby, once bright and laughing, turns her blind face to her mother, the pig-nose and ruined eyes hidden by her linen mask, and her voice, a thin ghost, whispers hoarsely from pale lips: "Do you remember how I danced once upon a time, mother? And chased the bright butterflies? I cannot remember what butterflies look like anymore. *I cannot remember.*"

No answer can I make, my lips are dumb as a dead woman's. The girls pass again, wraiths in black; I walk on into the darkness of the cloister, seeking the comfort of the confessional.

I have much to tell the priest of the sins for which one day I will pay in the presence of God:

I once tried to kill the King of England, and I have no regrets.

AUTHOR'S NOTES:

Juliane or Juliana, surnamed FitzRoy, de Breteuil or de Fontevraud was one of the many bastard children of Henry I. Possibly she was his eldest daughter. Little is known about her youth, although it is said her mother was called Ansfrida, which implies she may have been of Saxon heritage. Juliane most likely had a full brother, Richard of Lincoln, who was also favoured by Henry—he interceded with the King after Juliane's attempt on Henry's life. He died in the tragedy of the White Ship.

Little is known of the mid-section of Juliane's life so I had to be a bit creative here and build the story using the troubles that happened in Normandy at the time. So little was written about her that even the exact number of children she had is unknown. Several sources list only two boys and do not mention her two daughters, although they are the children mentioned by Orderic Vitalis as having their eyes put out by their grandfather. Certainly, there seems to be one son, William, who tried to gain back his parents' confiscated lands at a later date—but that is all that is known about him; there are no records of marriage or children, and it might be presumed he died quite young, without issue. There is nothing at all on the supposed other son, so again it is probable he died young, maybe in infancy. Of the girls, whose names are never given, their fate after their mutilation is also unclear—it is very likely that they were sent to a convent for their own safety. It may well have been Fontevraud, where Juliane retired after the death of her husband, Eustace.

The blinding and mutilation of Juliane's daughters is one of the saddest and most disturbing medieval tales—but it also shows the courage of a woman in defence of her children against her father and her King.

As usual, all songs and rhymes are medieval, although my translations.

If you have enjoyed this book, please leave a review!

OTHER WORKS BY J.P. REEDMAN

MEDIEVAL BABES SERIES:

MY FAIR LADY: ELEANOR OF PROVENCE, HENRY III'S LOST QUEEN

MISTRESS OF THE MAZE: Rosamund Clifford, Mistress of Henry II

THE CAPTIVE PRINCESS: Eleanor of Brittany, sister of the murdered Arthur, a prisoner of King John.

THE WHITE ROSE RENT: The short life of Katherine, illegitimate daughter of Richard III

THE PRINCESS NUN. Mary of Woodstock, Daughter of Edward I, the nun who liked fun!

RICHARD III and THE WARS OF THE ROSES:

I, RICHARD PLANTAGENET I: TANTE LE DESIREE. Richard in his own first-person perspective, as Duke of Gloucester

I, RICHARD PLANTAGENET II: LOYAULTE ME LIE. Second part of Richard's story, told in 1st person. The mystery of the Princes, the tragedy of Bosworth

A MAN WHO WOULD BE KING. First person account of Henry Stafford, Duke of Buckingham suspect in the murder of the Princes

SACRED KING—Historical fantasy in which Richard III enters a fantastical afterlife and is 'returned to the world' in a Leicester carpark

WHITE ROSES, GOLDEN SUNNES. Collection of short stories about Richard III and his family.

SECRET MARRIAGES. Edward IV's romantic entanglements with Eleanor Talbot and Elizabeth Woodville

BLOOD OF ROSES. Edward IV defeats the Lancastrians at Mortimer's Cross and Towton.

ROBIN HOOD:

THE HOOD GAME: RISE OF THE GREENWOOD KING. Robyn wins the Hood in an ancient midwinter rite and goes to fight the Sheriff and Sir Guy.

THE HOOD GAME; SHADOW OF THE BRAZEN HEAD. The Sheriff hunts Robyn and the outlaws using an animated prophetic brass head. And there's a new girl in the forest…

STONEHENGE:

THE STONEHENGE SAGA. Huge epic of the Bronze Age. Ritual, war, love and death. A prehistoric GAME OF STONES.

OTHER:

MY NAME IS NOT MIDNIGHT. Dystopian fantasy about a young girl in an alternate world Canada striving against the evil Sestren.

A DANCE THROUGH TIME. Time travel romance. Isabella falls through a decayed stage into Victorian times.

THE IRISH IMMIGRANT GIRL. Based on a true story. Young Mary leaves Ireland to seek work…but things don't go as expected.

ENDELIENTA, KINSWOMAN OF KING ARTHUR. Life story of the mysterious Cornish Saint and her magical White Cow.

…And many other short stories and novelettes…

Made in United States
North Haven, CT
22 October 2022

25785631R00114